Advance Praise

"Nina Berkhout has constructed a perfect pas de deux, where the characters dance deftly around the words they cannot bring themselves to say. *This Bright Dust*, the town of Grayley, and its remaining residents will stay with you long after you finish this book."
 — Russell Wangersky, author of *The Path of Most of Resistance*

"In *This Bright Dust*, Nina Berkhout's fading town of Grayley has been devastated by the Great Depression. Even for its loyal residents — skinny, haggard, and dwindling in number — it's a harsh place of droughts and blizzards, where grasshoppers chew through the curtains and the walls are dismantled for fuel. And yet! What a gentle, loving story this is, gracefully told, with a keen understanding of an earlier time. When the dust storm settles, you never know what you might find among the wild roses."
 — Kristen den Hartog, author of *And Me Among Them*

Also by NINA BERKHOUT

Fiction

Why Birds Sing

The Mosaic

The Gallery of Lost Species

Poetry

Elseworlds

Arrivals and Departures

Pas de Deux

This Way the Road

Letters from Deadman's Cay

NINA BERKHOUT

THIS BRIGHT DUST

a novel

Copyright © 2024 by Nina Berkhout.

All rights reserved. No part of this work may be reproduced or used in any form or by any means, electronic or mechanical, including photocopying, recording, or any retrieval system, without the prior written permission of the publisher or a licence from the Canadian Copyright Licensing Agency (Access Copyright). To contact Access Copyright, visit accesscopyright.ca or call 1-800-893-5777.

Edited by Bethany Gibson.
Copy edited by Peter Norman.
Cover and page design by Julie Scriver.

Cover image detailed from William Kurelek, *Bender Hamlet, the Farming Colony That Failed*, 1975, mixed media on board, 78.1 x 83.8 cm. © Copyright: the Estate of William Kurelek, courtesy of the Wynick/Tuck Gallery, Toronto.
Stamp motif in the section titles based on the commemorative stamp created by the Stovel Company Limited, Winnipeg, to mark the Royal Visit to Canada in 1939.
Printed in Canada by Marquis.
10 9 8 7 6 5 4 3 2 1

Library and Archives Canada Cataloguing in Publication
Title: This bright dust : a novel / Nina Berkhout.
Names: Berkhout, Nina, 1975- author.
Identifiers: Canadiana (print) 2024039383X | Canadiana (ebook) 20240393856 | ISBN 9781773104164 (softcover) | ISBN 9781773104171 (EPUB)
Subjects: LCGFT: Novels.
Classification: LCC PS8553.E688 T45 2024 | DDC C813/.6—dc23.

Goose Lane Editions acknowledges the generous support of the Government of Canada, the Canada Council for the Arts, and the Government of New Brunswick.

Goose Lane Editions is located on the unceded territory of the Wəlastəkwiyik whose ancestors along with the Mi'kmaq and Peskotomuhkati Nations signed Peace and Friendship Treaties with the British Crown in the 1700s.

Goose Lane Editions
500 Beaverbrook Court, Suite 330
Fredericton, New Brunswick
CANADA E3B 5X4
gooselane.com

For my mother and father

Our hoard is little, but our hearts are great.
—Alfred, Lord Tennyson, *Idylls of the King*

The roar fell faint and farther off, and soon
Sank to a foolish humming in our ears,
Like crickets in the long, hot afternoon
Among the wheat fields of the olden years.
—John McCrae, "The Unconquered Dead"

Winter 1939

1

As the sun broke open on the frozen prairie, Abel Dodds looked out the kitchen window. He saw his past in two buildings, which lay southeast of his fields, in a direction he no longer travelled.

The most distant building was the Wishart farm. His old classmate Una Wishart lived there with her son and grandfather, and her brother, Jake. Between Abel's house and hers lay the second building. The schoolhouse — a solitary whitewashed structure that stirred up unwanted feelings — appeared to float on the plain like a boat on an icy ocean.

He preferred to avoid both the Wishart farm and the schoolhouse. The Wisharts were busy enough that he did not often see them. He was mostly alone, which suited him fine. Up until the previous week, that was, when Jake stopped by on the pretext of wishing Abel a happy new year.

What have I gotten myself into, he now thought, drinking his coffee as the day's first light lengthened on the snow-encrusted dirt.

Jake had said that he was again headed south to work as a ranch hand. Feeding another man's livestock hay through the cold months, as he had done three years running. Ranch pay was decent, and Jake had experience managing stock. As did Abel. Many farmers in the area had once experimented in mixed farming, growing crops and raising cattle.

Winters past, when Jake had gone off ranching, a farmhand had stayed on at the Wishart bunkhouse to assist. Sometimes those fellows came over, asking to borrow tools, and Abel obliged and sent them on their way. Jake hadn't said as much, but Abel guessed that retaining a handyman was a luxury they couldn't afford anymore. And since Abel was the only other one around Grayley who hadn't packed it in for the mines, or the Okanagan, or Peace River — besides the Peloquins, who were currently off trapping — he supposed Jake had no choice but to call on him.

"What's keeping you here, Dodds?" Jake had asked, tobacco bulging from his lower lip as he leaned against the barn door.

The question Abel asked himself daily, and asked himself again now. Why did he stick around during these unproductive months?

He didn't bother explaining to Jake that what kept him from ranching was the memory of what he'd done in 1935. Like other farmers who had to kill off their starving cattle, Abel had slaughtered his own twelve dairy cows.

He had betrayed the cows' trust. Enticing them out of the barn with a bundle of hay, which he held under their noses. One by one they followed Abel into the pasture, and he positioned them to take his shot.

Jake had done away with the Wisharts' beef cattle too. Back when it happened, Abel's neighbour remained unfazed, saying he would bring stock in again when the time was right. In fact, Jake's plans became more grandiose as things got worse. But after walking through his own pasture of carcasses, great brown eyes staring up at him, imploring, Abel decided, *Never again*. He did not have the stomach for such carnage, and from then on only worked the land. When his collie died the year after the culling, Abel did not replace him. He would not take on more animals.

Of course, he still cared for Tansy and Elizabeth Moon, who had been with him a long time. Who were his family, really. And the

Winter, 1939

five chickens, for their eggs. But he did not want to tend to others' livestock. This was why he did not winter away.

Over the years, Abel had tried to work elsewhere in the off season. He had worked in the city, the factories and the mines. He had travelled from farm to farm, repairing tractors, barns and fences. And always, within weeks, he returned home.

He'd had other opportunities for leaving. After his father passed. And more recently, each time the bank offered to help him sell the farm at auction. There had also been one chance, years back. A moment which could have changed his circumstances and the course of his life, which he no longer reflected upon that often.

Reaching for his father's infantry binoculars on the sill, he focused on the Wishart property in time to see Jake emerge from the stable and saddle his temperamental stallion, and thought to himself, *Why did I say yes to him?*

Then again, how could he decline? Knowing that he and the Wisharts were the last ones left for miles. Knowing that, now that Grayley was officially unincorporated, Mounties would check in less. Knowing how supplies were dwindling.

There had been no way to refuse a neighbourly favour.

He had given Jake his word that he would look in—on Una, and her son, and their grandfather—making sure they managed through winter, though he wished instead that he were saddling Tansy and heading off to Albion Ranch himself.

Maybe they wouldn't come to him. Knowing Una Maeve Wishart, she would decline help even if it was sorely needed. Convincing himself of this, Abel felt better. He set down the binoculars and finished his coffee as daybreak sharpened the landscape to a postcard stillness.

On clear days, his whole life was contained within the kitchen window's frame. Beyond his fields, the east-west railway line and the primary road parallel to it ran across his view. Horseshoe River was there too, meandering around farmsteads, its eroded, dried-out bed sunken out of sight.

At the window's left edge—eastward—lay the schoolhouse and the Wishart farm, a quarter mile from his. And the Peloquins, another quarter mile east. At the window's right edge—westward—lay the town and railway station, and a little further, the grain elevators.

The station had an increasingly sparse timetable of passenger trains. When cargo trains rumbled by, few rail riders jumped off, word having gotten around that there was nothing here for them anymore.

Along the track, the uninhabited town of Grayley emerged from the dim, including the gaping hole on First Street where the church and hall burnt down three summers ago. Services took place in Sterling now, where both the Catholics and Protestants had set down roots. The popular Saturday night dances, which had drawn people from nearby communities, were no more.

One street over from First lay Main Street's abandoned storefronts. Grayley's population had never exceeded a hundred, but they had once had a grocer and butcher, diner and pool hall, telephone and post office, and blacksmith and hardware. All boarded up since '37.

To Abel's left and right, the sum total of his reality was spaced within walking distance. Like worn charms on a chain laid flat on a table. The railway was the chain holding everything together.

Looking east again, he watched Jake and his horse dissolve in the morning light.

He moved away from the window to turn on the radio. Warming his porridge on the stove, he sat at the table awaiting the news hour, and made a list of what needed doing after breakfast.

The announcer talked of Franco's offensive against Catalonia, and how the German Reich was building up their navy, while American physicists were studying uranium fission. Then came the report on volatile crop prices, and parliamentary sessions resuming late on account of the prime minister feeling unwell.

"Fool," Abel muttered.

Winter, 1939

He didn't know why he kept listening. Lately the radio only made him mad.

Like others desperate to believe in something, he had thought William Lyon Mackenzie King would rescue the prairies. But nothing prospered around Grayley since Mackenzie King had been re-elected. Banks kept collecting, evicting farmers and displacing families. Politicians were asses, the lot of them.

He rose to turn the radio off as the announcer launched into details of the Royal Tour.

Abel paused, fingers on the dial.

The king and queen of England were to arrive in Canada in spring. Their itinerary had just been released. They would cross the country by train, making stops here and there and everywhere, visiting Montreal and Toronto and Winnipeg, seeing big cities and small towns and nature's splendours, passing through the prairies, then the Rockies and Vancouver. There was even talk of a detour through the United States. And the prime minister would travel with them.

Abel could not believe what he was hearing.

Nothing would ever change, despite government promises. First that buffoon R.B. Bennett, now bizarre Mackenzie King, who had all but forgotten the drought and made declarations as if everything had gone back to normal. Who had been quoted saying of the West, "I doubt if it will be of any real use again." And who was now focusing his attention on a royal visit while Grayley blew away, dust to dust.

Abel clicked the radio off as a train approached.

Returning to the kitchen window to watch the passing cars, he felt the loneliness of the locomotive's call as it barrelled over the crossroads. He had watched thousands of trains go by as he stood on the oval rug he had braided himself from linen, wool and burlap strips. He leaned over the deep sink whose rusting metal was visible in patches under the chipped enamel coating, the hand pump disconnected from the empty cistern outside.

Abel imagined himself a passenger, leaving everything behind just like the farmers who had up and vanished, their tumbledown houses scattered across the fields like artifacts. In his reinvented existence, he felt far from Cutland County already. But then, there was that greater part of him. Wanting to stay.

Within seconds the rumbling locomotive and its railcars moved on.

And would move on until they left the whole of the parched prairies behind.

Heading outside, he faced his neighbour's grey house. Smoke drifted from the chimney like a feather. A rough-legged hawk circled in silence above the plain. Una Wishart's home glowed in the early sun. As though it had pulled into itself all the light around it, from the earth, the road, and the endless fields that had long ago lost their colour. It glowed as though it contained the light of the whole world. He would have liked to write a poem then. But he had much to do and daylight would not last long.

Reaching for his axe to break ice off the trough by the barn, he heard a child's voice carried on the wind. Turning, he saw Una's son bounding from the schoolhouse, leaping down the steps and into the dirt yard with the regulation strap, chasing Russian thistle and kicking it around like a ball. From afar he had observed the boy grow for years. Watched him running through the fields or along the rail line to town, clutching a basket for selling eggs or for buying provisions. If the boy waved, Abel waved back. Nothing more. His mother had likely warned him not to visit.

In October, Abel had witnessed the headmaster rush out of the schoolhouse, hurrying with his suitcase toward the station as the morning train approached. Within minutes the young man was on the platform, then boarding without a backward glance.

Over the past twelve months a succession of teachers had quickly returned east. They had tired of gifts of milk and preserves in lieu of pay. They would no longer work for IOUs. By November no ratepayers or pupils remained, besides the Wishart boy. The school shut down for good before Christmas, when Grayley's mayor, station agent, grain elevator operator and last few farmers also departed.

A long time ago, inside that small building, Abel had attended school with between forty and fifty children, depending on the year, from surrounding farms.

The boy made a game of whipping the tumbleweed. When the wind picked up, he crouched, thwacking the ground with his piece of leather. He then ran up the steps to ring the bell. Abel couldn't hear the clapper hit the mouth over the sound of the wind — it was a light, small bell — but knew the gesture. As a child, he had been granted permission to ring it himself and still recalled the feel of the coarse rope, just as he remembered every inch of the schoolhouse interior, though he hadn't been inside again since the great failure of his final days there.

Making his way to the barn, he caught sight of Tansy sauntering toward the boy.

She must have nudged open her stall gate and slipped through the loose stable door. She moved slowly, and could be drawn back with a peppermint, but still — of all mornings, when he needed to make use of the good weather to patch the roof, and clean the binder he hadn't done a proper job of cleaning before storing last fall, and apparently now mend a gate — why today of all days did his truant mare have to be lured away, her pace picking up to a trot. She could never resist a little fun, especially when she knew chores awaited. Retrieving her halter and lead from a post, he started after her.

> "U" like a horseshoe and "n"
> a rainbow, "a" like the alphabet's
> first letter committed to memory.
> —A.D.

2

A Chinook arch spread over the sky like a cow rib. Within hours icicles would drip, crackle and fall from rooftops. Within the day, waves of warm wind would eat the thin layer of snow off the fields, exposing the soil to bugs and disease.

The mild air was a respite from the cold, though.

Early January, and it had been a long winter already. September frosts had ruined unharvested crops. Killing what sense of possibility the community had been clinging to — after eight long years of drought and black blizzards — that their wheat, which had ripened late, would yield bountiful grain, as they'd heard had happened through southern parts of the province. For those who had stuck it out, 1938 was the year things were meant to improve. But they hadn't. At least not around Grayley.

Abel supposed this was why everyone left.

Catching up with his horse, he walked with her the rest of the way to the school. The boy was sitting on the steps, and stared at him as he approached.

After all these years, Abel still felt self-conscious entering the schoolyard, about his appearance and his stammer, for which he had been mercilessly teased.

His too long, crooked nose lent his face an ungainly asymmetry. He had an under-bite and thin lips, and acne-scarred cheeks—as though someone had taken a chisel to his mug, Jake Wishart once said. His prominent ears, high forehead and deep-set eyes all became more pronounced during his final school years. As Abel grew from childhood to adolescence to adulthood, his ugliness grew with him. His speech problems, too, had worsened with age.

Handsome or not, as his father often told him, he could do everything that needed doing. He could run a farm. And think, feel, laugh and cry like any other.

The Wishart boy was pale. Beneath his patched, oversized sweater he seemed frail as he squinted into the wind. Abel heard he'd been sick. "Toby, is it?" he asked. "I just— came to see if everything's alright. Your un-un— Jake asked me to look in. While he's away."

"We don't need anyone lookin' in."

"'Course not."

Abel glanced past Toby to the Dutch door behind him, its swing bar hanging down from the hinge. "Your mom know you're here?"

"It's her who kicked me out," Toby answered, his voice raspy. "Says she'll teach me herself once she gets around to it. Else I'm to pick field rocks all winter."

The Wisharts' rusted, engineless truck was a permanent fixture in their yard, anchored by sand. Their team of horses could not have pulled it without it crumbling to pieces. Without a snowplane or automobile, the boy wouldn't make it to the school in Sterling and back within a day. Then again, with the dissolution of Grayley, school was no longer compulsory for him, there being no learning establishment within three miles.

"Is it you who— chased the last headmaster off?"

"Never learned squat from him. Good riddance."

Winter, 1939

Abel thought how alike the boy was to his mother, his eyes bluing deeper as his small face reddened.

"Besides," he tried spitting in the dirt, then wiped his mouth on his arm, "there's no need to finish."

The boy knew the Attendance Act, then.

"Your mom finished," Abel said. "She won the Cut-Cutland County scholarship in our day. Which was something."

"She says Aunt Brynn's the cleverest." He brought one knee up and rested his chin on it. "She's in training. To be a nurse."

A year behind him, Abel had never gotten to know Una's sister, Brynn. He only remembered her as loud and insolent. She wore lipstick and ran around with kids from town. Upon graduation she left Grayley, never to return. Unlike Una, who had come back.

Toby got up and approached Tansy, stroking her dapple-grey coat, faded now to near white.

Abel rubbed his knuckles. "How old are you?"

Toby stood a little taller. "Almost eight."

Had that many years gone by already, since Una had gone off to university?

Abel could still see her standing on the platform with her trunk, in her gloves and straw hat, waving goodbye. The whole town had come to see her off, himself included. He never understood why she had reappeared, a year and a half later, with a baby. Why she had given up everything to return to nothing.

The boy cocked his head. "How old are *you*?"

"Almost twenty-seven."

"Is it true they used to call you Doleful Dodds?"

Abel nodded, and waited, but no further insults were proffered.

Toby tried climbing Tansy. It took a while, but he managed to get on sidesaddle, then astride.

Abel peered up at his old school again. "What's it—like in there?"

"Go and see for yourself." Toby scratched Tansy's neck behind the ear.

"That's alright."

"What a pudding-heart!"

Ignoring the taunt, Abel let go of Tansy's rein. Removing his hat, he climbed the steps and turned the door's brass knob. As he passed through the bare cloakroom, his heart pounded — a familiar sensation from being in school.

He was having a hard time reconciling his memories with the decrepit space he now found himself in. Certainly the depression had hit the prairies hardest. But how had Grayley come to this, and how had the school board neglected to provide assistance?

The pot-bellied stove in the back corner was cold to the touch, the coal bucket empty at its side. Gone were the days of inkwells and proper desks, which Abel thought had likely been burned for heat. Half-broken apple crates, delivered by train along with other handouts, served as seats and writing surfaces.

He walked up to the headmaster's desk in front of the chalkboard, black but for the ghostly alphabet snaking across its top — the same upper and lowercase letters, he was sure, scrawled there by his own teacher, Miss Kitty, long ago.

Above the chalk alphabet, the faint outline of a tiny rose Miss Kitty had drawn above the Z was miraculously still visible. A depiction of a bud like the wild roses that once bloomed along Horseshoe River, back when water flowed between its banks.

Other than the rose, the only thing decorating the room was George VI's portrait on the wall. Casting his gaze eternally upon the bleak space. The reluctant sovereign, they called him. The one who stuttered. That was all Abel knew about the king of Canada.

Bringing two crates together, he sat.

The last time he'd been inside the school had been during provincial exams, close to ten years ago. How he had studied! Sleeping in the barn at night, learning theorems by light of the kerosene lamp while tending to newborn calves. Rising with his books a good hour before chores. Memorizing laws of physics while shovelling shit and furrowing. His father, who left school after grade six—content with his reading and basic numbers—could not make sense of it, but told him that his mother would have been proud.

All that final year Miss Kitty had said, "Abel, you will go on to do great things." She even came for tea once, and told Gilly Dodds that his son had enough smarts to attend university in the provincial capital. A scholarship was available—only one for the school, granted annually—and he held the highest grades. With exams, he could win.

The pink rising to his cheeks, his father pre-emptively told Abel he'd manage without him. "It's your decision, son. If you leave, give your best effort. If you leave, live with passion and acknowledge sin." Not long after, Gilly Dodds went away. And here Abel still was, larger in body but not in mind.

Abel's thoughts turned to war. The old one his father served in, and the new one looming.

Besides crop yields, no one talked about anything else anymore. After last harvest, at the foot of the empty grain elevators, the few remaining farmers argued over what Mackenzie King had planned for Canada's role if it came down to a war, and whether Hitler and Mussolini would join forces. Should the government support Britain or assert its independence? Abel followed his father's view. Even as a veteran, Gilly Dodds had believed that Canada should stay out of overseas conflicts. But his father also told him that "once we're in, we're in." Abel didn't participate in these debates. He had enough to keep his mind awake at night. What good was worrying when no one knew what would come to pass?

He tried his best to keep focused on the task at hand: getting through winter. Nonetheless the radio and the newspapers he insulated the walls with sometimes drew him in, with stories of foreboding from around the world. Stories of people being rounded up, and families fleeing Europe. Every month brought more photographs of the Nazi emblem and flag. It seemed that days darker than the last decade of storms and famine were coming.

The Chinook blew ice crystals against the windowpanes, which were cracked in intersecting lines. Abel rose from his crate and returned outside.

The Wishart boy was already wandering off. He had tied Tansy to the hitching rail where Abel and so many others used to leave their snowshoes, horses and wagons.

Abel unknotted Tansy's lead. She blinked slowly, her long lashes tipped silver, her mane tangling in the wind.

She had been with him twenty years.

The first year after his father returned from the war, the harvest was golden. He brought home many gifts. Floral dresses and a washing machine for his mother. A telephone, a new John Deere and a Model T. Then, on Abel's birthday, this speckled foal born at the Peloquins' appeared in the paddock. "She's yours," his father told him. "Take care of her."

Once the creditors began calling, Gilly Dodds insisted everything go but his son's horse. As two bulky repossession agents led Tansy away, he gave them a good-natured talking-to. They had the war in common. Could they not grant a fellow Canuck this one kindness?

In the trade-off, Gilly lost his Lee-Enfield rifle. Under fire on the battlefield, he'd chanced upon the gun and plucked it from the mud after tossing aside his own jammed-up Ross. That split-second decision had saved his life, and the rifle had come home with him as a prized possession — and now it was gone. But Tansy stayed on.

Stroking her shoulders, Abel directed his sight down the rail line to where Grayley's three grain elevators stood on the edge of town. The Wise Men, his father called them, back when each one overflowed with grain. Hollowed out, they were leaning and would soon fall.

His mare stepped back and raised her head, pulling her lead. He watched Toby's diminishing figure trudging along, head low.

Abel turned homeward. The Chinook wouldn't last. He needed

Winter, 1939

to use these days of warmth to tackle as many chores as possible before temperatures plunged again.

He had worked harder than ever this past year, while all around wild grasses reclaimed deserted croplands. Even the suitcase farmers who purchased land on the cheap, who used to come from the city and camp out in the fields for summer and fall reaping, hadn't appeared in years. Rumours had circulated. About those who had vanished. A lot involved people having to rob necessities from stores and warehouses to get by, or suicides and murders — husbands killing their wives and children, then themselves, when they could no longer provide. He was so goddamn tired of the rumours.

Yet looking out at the vast stretch of country etched with snow filled him with an inner peace like nothing else did — except maybe one person, long ago — and something in him was certain that it was only a matter of time before his farm thrived again.

While others said why bother, Abel had never stopped trying to bring his plot of wind-eroded soil back to life. He didn't know if this was stubbornness or stupidity.

The fall yield had been meagre. The little grain he reaped barely paid for its planting. But like every other drought-afflicted cycle, he had ploughed, seeded and harvested. Then seeded again, for the first time, with winter wheat. There wasn't much he could do in the fields now, not until spring. Not much besides watch and wait, for whatever nature had in store.

Tansy balked. Abel nudged her along, thinking how Elizabeth Moon would soon be uncomfortable with a full udder. After milking, he would start on retying those bundles of hay where mice had chewed the strings. And he would need to take the radio battery out to the pitted Wincharger while it was still spinning — one more task to add to the day's list. He thought about Toby Wishart. He glanced over his shoulder, but couldn't see the boy anymore.

He gave Tansy a peppermint and led his mare homeward.

Inside the stable, his cow greeted them with a bellow. Once the milking was done, Abel pulled the door shut and checked the coop, feeding the chickens some worthless, shrunken grain. He gathered three eggs. The hens were hardly laying. They needed greater warmth and longer daylight.

It was early evening by the time he got around to securing the stall gate and fixing the stable door. He was tightening a latch, swinging it to and fro, when he saw her.

She was headed for the schoolhouse. He stopped his work as Una Wishart crossed the fields. Above her, a crescent moon rose in the purplish-blue sky like a comma without words.

> *I dream of a life with you*
> *where dust turns to swallows*
> *and we speak freely.*
> —A.D.

3

Abel stored the snow that fell. So little of it had come down in recent winters, and sometimes none fell at all, the earth seemingly caught in an arid chokehold. Now that the cold was back, a few inches of white blew in, which he scooped into as many barrels as he could patch.

He knew the Wisharts were doing the same, the wells around Grayley having long ago gone dry, along with Horseshoe River, and the nearby creeks and sloughs. Everyone in Cutland County had mastered the art of water rationing, accumulating what they could for the stock, then bringing what remained inside for cooking, drinking and washing dishes. Using the same water to scrub clothes and, once the dirt settled, using that water to clean themselves.

When the snow stopped falling she crossed the fields again.

For over a week he observed Una, her son and grandfather visiting the schoolhouse.

From where he worked to salvage rotted wood shingles on his roof, he had a good view of the Wishart home to the southeast.

Their parcels of land shared the same design. Their houses were simple and went up quickly, and consisted of a one-floor frame structure of wood siding with a sloped roof. Each property also had a paddock, stable, implements shed, coop and privy. Right down to the fieldstone foundations and plain porcelain doorknobs, their farms matched. The only difference was that Abel had a large barn for dairy cows, empty, and the Wisharts had a small sagging barn, which gave way to a bunkhouse, an old sod house and a dreary grazing area where beef cattle once roamed.

While Abel removed decayed portions of shingles with a hatchet, coating the pieces he saved with a mixture of oil and sawdust, early afternoons Una led the way across the plain, scarf whipping behind her, advancing through the white landscape like a ghost.

Once there, she swept the steps and raised the Canadian Red Ensign. Then she rang the bell, holding her shawl tight against the wind as she ushered Toby and her grandfather inside.

Abel wondered whether to check if she needed anything. Then quickly decided it best to leave her be. She had always been strong-willed. She could more than take care of herself.

Only he never saw smoke rising from the schoolhouse chimney, and usually within an hour or two the family headed home. Meaning—he imagined—the cold was unbearable, even for her.

The sun hit the thickening clouds, illuminating the small building before the clouds obscured the light again, and the prairie went grey.

The more he thought about the Wisharts' discomfort, the more distracted he got up on the roof as he patched holes with tar and sacking, face prickling in the biting air. He should go and see if the windows were sealed, at least. And fix the broken Dutch door. It was late morning. He could stop drafts with newsprint and rags before they began their afternoon session.

He set his supplies back into the gallon can—the one his father once brought home filled with peaches—and climbed down the

Winter, 1939

ladder to where Tansy waited, tied to her picket post, her slow breaths visible at each exhale.

Blowing on his hands Abel massaged his mare's back, working his way deeper into the muscles as she half-closed her eyes. "I'll get this over with." He took her into the paddock. "So we can go back to our routine."

It was freezing in the classroom, the cast iron stove still empty. The building had no electricity. All of Grayley lay beyond electrification, though the utility company had intended power for the township in 1929, mere weeks before Black Tuesday.

Someone had drawn a sun on the board. A chalky sun and nothing else to warm them. Approaching the bookshelf, he pulled out mouldy readers whose contents were no longer legible. Pages dropped in clumps to the floor as he opened them. Without textbooks, he wondered what Una was teaching. As for the teacher's desk, its drawers were empty, aside from an old Eaton's catalogue. Sitting in the swivel chair, he flipped through it, lingering over the farm implements pages.

Then he passed through to the teacherage, forcing the door to the back room open with his shoulder. The living quarter was dank, a blanket draped over the curtain rod above a single window. When he threw the blanket onto the straw bed, the room brightened, revealing meagre furnishings: a washstand, a small table and a chair with a broken back. He found matches in the table drawer, built a fire and lit the wood-burning stove by the back door leading to the privy, thinking to send more warmth to the front room. But the few logs stacked against the wall were damp. Ignited, they filled the teacher's quarters with smoke before fizzling out.

He opened the cupboard onto a nest of mice. With a sweep of the broom he tossed them out the teacherage door for the hawks or the cold to claim. For a moment, he looked down the rail line he once walked as a boy, picking saskatoon berries all the way past town, the station and the grain elevators. The track appeared as an endless ladder. Often, he had pictured himself lifting the whole thing up through the air, climbing the rails to infinity.

From where he stood he could also see the old general store, where his father bought him licorice twists and jawbreakers. And the cemetery next to the burnt church on First Street, containing his parents' snow-capped stones. It was where he himself, he supposed, would be buried one day, beneath pennycress weeds.

Locating the janitor's toolbox in the utility cupboard by the chalkboard, he flattened some empty soup cans from the countertop, and sought out those areas in the walls where flecks of sun streamed in, wedging the tin in place. Then he repaired the apple crates that were broken.

He was stuffing newsprint around the sills when he saw them coming.

At first he wanted to go. But out in the open they'd see him running, and how would that look? He took a deep breath and stayed put.

Una's grandfather came in first.

Since Abel could remember, it was Merle Wishart raising Jake, Una and Brynn. Abel had little memory of Una's parents, taken by the sickness brought back by soldiers after the Great War. Same as his own mother. He hardly remembered her anymore, either. In his mind it had always been just him and his father, since he was six or seven. If ever he did manage to glimpse Evangeline Dodds in his recollections, mostly it was inside something else. Glimmers of light on walls or the liquid song of wrens. Drifts of her voice, and laughter, intermingling with his father's.

Merle's sheepskin coat was worn to holes at the elbows, and hung loosely over his curved frame. He stooped as he walked in. As though an anchor was moored to his chest, pulling his whole aspect downward, including his eyes, earlobes and long grey moustache.

Winter, 1939

He was the opposite of bowlegged. Not knock-kneed, Abel didn't think, but his limbs all bent the wrong way. Was there a name for that? Joint problems, something to do with arthritis. The way he moved reminded Abel of a broken weathervane. He didn't appear out in the fields much anymore. When Abel saw him, those days he scanned the horizon with his father's binoculars, Merle could be spotted puttering around the barn or the bunkhouse, doing odd jobs with his great-grandson trailing behind.

He tipped his hat at Abel. "I heard you were the only other one dumb enough to stick around. Been meaning to call on you." He pulled a crate out and sat. "Never made it past grade four. Figured I could do with some learnin'."

Clutching a toy airplane, Toby burst in, running past his great-grandfather and calling, "Told you we had a trespasser."

Una Maeve walked in then.

Abel hadn't truly spoken with her since their school days. Back when she sat in the middle front row seat, and he sat directly behind her. Sure, a few times yearly they bumped into each other at the town hall, or community gatherings, the odd time he would go. In those awkward moments they exchanged hasty greetings. But that was all.

He had always felt a crippling shyness around her. No matter how chatty she was toward him. He experienced this with a renewed intensity after she went off to school, and came back with a son. At first, she had approached him. She wore a sling in which the child slept, and conversed in her usual, affable way. But he was so flummoxed by her return that he could not reciprocate. He kept his distance, and eventually she did too. Their avoidance became mutual.

It dawned on Abel that up until now, the wider population of Grayley had diverted them from each other. All those extra folk scattered between them like sheaves, shielding him. Now it was just them left.

"Oh!" Her face fell. "It's you."

"I came to see"—Abel swallowed—"if anything's needed."

She wore layers of skirts, one over the other, and fingerless gloves. Her dark hair still had that blue shine, like the feathers of a grackle or a cowbird. But it was short now, which made her neck seem longer than before. And her face was less full, which made her eyes seem bigger, blue-green. He felt briefly disoriented as she stared at him, and looked down at his boots, which were lined with cardboard soles.

"I thought you were Lewis," she said.

Lewis Lyte, she meant, their former schoolmate turned Mountie, who sometimes stopped by on his rounds, and to deliver mail.

When Abel looked up, she was at the cubby table beneath the portrait of King George. Retrieving the folded flag from the top shelf, she made her way outside again. "We're fine," she called from the cloakroom in her light, singsong voice. "Aren't we, boys?"

Toby and Merle swapped a furtive glance. She came back in, checking the clock on the wall opposite the king. The clock was a new addition to the room, mounted at a low enough height to be wound by children, though the key was missing, the lens gone, the short and long hands set permanently on noon or midnight.

"I'll just—" Abel knelt and gathered his hammered tins. "I'll finish."

Removing Toby's toque and wiping his hair off his forehead, Una shrugged as if to say *suit yourself*. Then she turned and wrote the date, January 17, 1939, on the board.

They all kept their coats on. As Una clasped her hands and began the lesson, her breath came out in huffs. Abel half-listened, plugging holes with the last bits of tin.

No matter her prompts to her boy—Can you tell me about the Winnipeg General Strike? Who are the Famous Five? What's a relief camp? Shall we recite the periodic table?—her student remained downcast. Toby fidgeted and looked away. As for Merle, he lowered his hat over his eyes to doze.

Winter, 1939

She picked the mail-order catalogue up off the desk. "How about we work out some arithmetic from Eaton's?"

"We can't afford any of that." Toby hugged his knees.

"I suppose you're right." She set it back down. "How silly of me."

If only, Abel thought, she had Miss Kitty to guide her.

At the start of each school year, their teacher had gone from desk to desk, spending a few minutes with each student to uncover their interests. She then taught them more about these subjects. Abel's interest, which he tried to keep secret from his schoolmates, was poetry. With poetry, he didn't pause or stammer. When Miss Kitty had discovered a verse jotted on his reader—he had been careless enough to write on the inside cover—she kept him after class. Though he denied writing it, she told him, "Keep at your pocket poems. Even if they're just a few lines. Carry them with you. Wherever you go."

Sometimes he still wrote. Not often. But sometimes.

Toby raised his arm.

"Yes, Tobias?" Una brightened.

He blinked. "Are the Germans coming to kill us?"

Una pressed her lips together. She glanced above the board, where once had been a pulldown map. Erasing the chalk sun, she drew a crude map of Europe. "In fact, the National Socialist Party has started to threaten a lot of countries." She circled Germany and the Rhineland.

Toby shrank in his seat. Merle lifted his hat up off his face and raised an eyebrow at his granddaughter. The boy tossed his plane at his mother.

Picking it up off the floor and setting it on his desk, Una shook a finger at him. "Count yourself lucky. In Hitler's world, a lot of children don't get to go to school anymore." She sighed. Then she straightened and wrote on the board: Sudetenland, Austria, Czechoslovakia. "Let's start with invasions."

Talk of imminent hostilities filled Abel with dread as he assessed the half-drawn map.

Toby worked at removing a splinter from his thumb. Una looked from her growing list of regions and countries to her son, eventually putting her chalk down and shaking her head. "This won't do."

She wiped the board and drew Europe once more, adding England, the sea and North America. Then she traced a dotted line from Great Britain across the ocean, to the province of Quebec.

When she finished, she approached the king's portrait, studying it a moment before pulling a dishcloth from her pocket and reaching up to rub a smudge off his chin. She polished the glass clean and turned back to her family. "Did you hear?" she said. "The king and queen are coming."

Toby looked up from his plane. "Coming to Grayley?"

Abel hammered a last piece of tin in place while she paused as if considering, then nodded. "The Royal Tour will cross the whole country." Returning to the board, she extended her dotted line from Quebec to British Columbia. "They arrive in spring."

Toby's arm went up again. Where would their majesties sleep? What would they eat? Were the princesses coming too?

"I imagine they'll sleep in their carriage," Una replied. "I'm sure there will be a chef on board."

Merle Wishart sat up and observed his great-grandson, a slow smile forming on his grizzled face. "We've never had a reigning king visit Canada before."

Abel stared hard at the portrait on the dingy wall. "It's pr-propaganda. This tour. They— know they've lost favour. Besides, they won't— stop at a derelict town like ours."

His words seemed to startle the Wisharts. As if they'd forgotten he was there.

He could not say what got into him, speaking out like that. He hadn't intended to contradict her before her family the way they used to counter each other in Miss Kitty's class, like a couple of headstrong mules. Why, when he saw Una, did he always feel the need to oppose her? He did not know how to diffuse this tension with her. Yet he had missed their heated discussions. Heart banging in his chest like the barn door's iron ring in the wind.

Toby looked from Abel to his mother.

"Or it could simply be," Una said, "that Prime Minister Mackenzie King invited them. And declining would be rude."

"Do you know what this sp-spectacle will cost?" The back of Abel's neck burned. "Who's p-paying for this while we starve? It's not…"

She faced him, hands on hips. "Not what?"

"Not— part of the curriculum."

She tilted her head back and laughed. Her laughter, like clouds of birds.

Toby's lower lip quivered. "They won't stop at our lousy town. Will they?"

"I think we can all agree that we have a station and a platform. Though the wood may be a little rotted"—Una rubbed her son's back—"trains still pass by. Therefore, the Royal Train will come through Grayley. Because it must." She swallowed. "Isn't that right, grandad?"

Merle stood and went to the window. He shoved his hands deep into his coat pockets. "No other way to cross the land. Aside from these rails."

Toby cast a scornful eye at Abel. "But he said…"

"Pay him no mind." Una clenched her fists. "I'm telling you for certain, King George and Queen Elizabeth will call on us. And it's our duty to welcome them to Grayley as we would any other. No matter how long or short their stay, we're to treat them as our guests."

"He's got a stammer like you," Toby told Abel, "that king." The boy approached the teacher's desk and retrieved the Eaton's catalogue. "We'll need new clothes," he added. "If royalty's coming."

Abel could not listen to this nonsense. He put his hat on and took his leave, slamming the Dutch door fast so snow would not blow in.

Passing the flagpole, he looked up at the flag of the Dominion, then out at the Wishart farm. Clothing hung stiff on the line like frozen corpses.

By process of sublimation, the ice would evaporate from a solid state until everything eventually dried. This was what she should have explained today, he thought. Una should have taught her son about sublimation, and the disappearance of something into nothing.

Then again, he had to hand it to her for fabricating a tale she seemed to half-believe herself. She had played Miss Kitty's trick, figuring out what interested her pupil. Now she had to make it come true.

> *Always a train departing.*
> *What passes between us blurs*
> *in a cargo's speed of stars.*
> —*A.D.*

4

A passing train let out puffs of smoke like a dragon. Hearing the plaintive cries from within the stock cars, Tansy flicked her ears back. Abel petted her with rhythmic strokes until she was less nervous, remaining beside him while he worked.

He could still cut into the winter earth with his axe. The ground wasn't completely solid yet. Methodically he carved a hole, sifted through the dirt, then filled and flattened it, marking each spot with pebbles before moving on.

Swinging the axe down on the frigid soil, he thought about the alarming report from the evening before on Hitler's recent Reichstag speech, which made clear the chancellor's deranged vision for the world. He struck at the soil again and again until the axe split the field open. Kneeling, he brushed snow and sand aside until he loosened a flat stone. This one had a patterned surface different from the others. Flow lines, maybe, or a skeletal imprint. Standing, he put the finding into his pocket.

Then his axe wouldn't come out of the ground.

He tried lifting the handle. Rocking it up and down, and to and fro. But it wouldn't budge. After several attempts he laughed, shaking his head, and left the sharp tip buried.

The train cried out from afar. Tansy whinnied as if calling to the herd in the railcars. Abel whistled and she walked with him to the farmyard, where he led her to the stable, then headed indoors.

The house Gilly Dodds built, once a clean, bright white, had turned somber grey from exposure to years of hard weather. Abel hadn't repainted it since his father had died. Loose flakes clung to the wood siding like wings of butterflies.

His father had called their modest home "cozy." Abel supposed it was, in a rundown way. Though wind, and at times snow, came in through crevices where the sawed board walls shrank and separated in the bone-cold air, he managed to keep the front part of the house reasonably warm. On the other side of the wall, though, where both bedrooms lay, was glacial.

The furniture was arranged as it had been when Abel was a child. As long as he paid interest on the loan, the bank refrained from seizing household items. The radio was positioned in the corner of the living room, by the second of the house's two front windows framed by pillowcase curtains. It faced the upholstered sofa, whose stripes helped disguise tears in the blue fabric. Beside the sofa stood his father's walnut smoking table, and push-down ashtray holding Gilly Dodds' pipes, which Abel picked up to smell from time to time.

Before the sofa a cedar chest doubled as a low table and footrest. Inside the chest, bedding and linens worn out years prior had been replaced by credit agreements, account statements, promissory notes and receipts.

The rocker's place was by the stove, adapted to burn both coal and wood. The kitchen—an extension of the living room where plank floor turned to faded checkerboard linoleum—accommodated the old Hoosier cabinet containing his mother's recipe book and Bible, silverware, china plates. And a carnival glass dish which Abel filled

Winter, 1939

with Tansy's peppermints, supplied by Cy Peloquin, who obtained these in large quantities from his travelling salesman cousin.

The kitchen also held the square pine table with four chairs built by his father. Here Abel ate. And here he ran numbers late into the night, adding the last harvest's earnings then subtracting, dividing and further dividing amounts owed.

Other nights, overcome with tiredness, he sat in the rocker, closed his eyes and rested. Listening to the rhythmic chugging of trains.

Tossing coal mix into the firebox, he pulled open the stove's oven door to lay out his wet wool socks and gloves. Then he fried an egg and made coffee—a substitute mix his father invented for when they ran out of the real thing, concocted from hot water, chicory root, molasses, cornmeal and a drop of rosewater.

The stove still did a good job heating the room. All winter he dried out his woollen underthings on its racks. The circular lids were corroded but usable. The kettle was full of holes too. But he had his mother's iron pan, his father's percolator and a pot he was particularly proud of, which he'd fashioned from an oil drum.

His cooked meals usually consisted of eggs or rabbit. Rabbits were always plentiful, as gophers would be come spring. With most of the cattle gone from the region, beef was a thing of the past. Pork was hard to come by now as well, though he often imagined mouth-watering, succulent roasts as he cut into tough, boiled cubes of rabbit meat. The boiling removed the gamey taste. He boiled Russian thistle, too, to reduce its bitterness. Also, he had milk and butter from Elizabeth Moon. And from his meagre yield of pulverized wheat he made bread.

What he missed were vegetables. Nothing green would sprout. Nor would potatoes. Some nights he wished for nothing more than a whopping baked potato, but the ones he planted came out as small as his thumb.

On his fingernails were severe, raised ridges. Marks of poor nutrition, the doctor once told him in passing at the hardware, where

Abel had just spent his last coins on liniment and hoof conditioner for Tansy. At that time, he had come close to starvation, and contemplated a trip to the relief depot in the city. But he dismissed the thought of handouts quickly, cutting his nails extra short instead.

How could there not be enough food when Canada provided grain to the world!

It was as ludicrous as those trains sent to Saskatchewan years ago, full of food and clothing from easterners, including fine dining attire no one had any use for, and salt cod no one knew how to consume. Ottawa did not understand that these pity cargoes only served to further enrage the people of the prairies. Some accepted donations on account of their children, but many were insulted by the gesture. They needed jobs. They needed to keep their farms. Abel wasn't the only one who would rather rely on his own soil, or die trying, than take charity.

Had they sent wood instead of cod there would have been less outrage. He wondered if those in the land of trees knew how lucky they were. To have fuel at the ready, neatly stacked at their feet, with no need to go grubbing for dung and black rock. But then, he thought as he got up from the table with his dishes and stood at the kitchen window, easterners did not have this view.

He rinsed his cup, plate and fork in the bucket of grey water in the sink. Drying the dishes, he turned them upside down against the dust as he slid them into the cupboard—a habit even in winter, when there was no need to do so. Then he focused his binoculars on the schoolhouse as Una came out, swept the steps of snow and raised the flag. Her son tried making snowballs but the snow was dry. He threw it loose against the building. The wind lifted the powder, carrying it away.

They were so thin. What were they eating? The Wisharts had a couple of horses and chickens, but Jake had butchered their dairy cow last winter. He'd seen Merle walking the treeless expanse carrying rabbits by the hind legs, and once, a game strap of blackbirds. Probably they had preserves and shrivelled vegetables in the old sod house, which Toby skipped in and out of daily. But how soon before their stores were depleted?

Una waved her son inside. Abel felt a sharp longing then for his school days.

After the Dutch door closed, he rested the binoculars on the sill next to a pair of ceramic, winged pigs. His father had won the plump figurines one year at the county fair. Empty of salt and pepper, they still cheered Abel. Polishing them with his sleeve, he set them back in place and studied his appearance. He didn't need a mirror to know what he looked like. On days the window reflected light, he saw clearly. His clothing hadn't been replaced in years. His father would be appalled that he didn't keep himself tidy, failing to wash and bathe weekly.

Combing back his silt-brown hair with his fingers, he addressed the pigs. "I am ugly," he told them. "And I will always be ugly, and there is no use lamenting this."

But he could at least make himself respectable.

Wiping clean the porridge pot, he stepped outside and scooped snow from a low drift along the side of the house. Returning inside with the heaping pot, the snow shrinking as it melted on the stove, he retrieved his father's razor, sharpening it on the old strop. Once the water warmed, he topped off the bucket in the kitchen sink, scrubbing his rough skin with a thin cake of soap. Then he shaved his face, cut his hair and brushed his teeth with baking soda.

His shirt was so worn it was transparent. He counted four holes. The shirt had belonged to his father, the rest of his clothing having gone to Cy Peloquin, since it was too tight on Abel. He had kept his father's tan cowboy hat, though, and still wore it. The inside leather sweatband was wrinkled and too soft, but the felt crown and brim held their shape enough to protect him from the elements.

The family's one bedroom dresser still contained a few of his parents' belongings, including their wedding bands, and his father's suspenders and pocket watch. His mother's shawl pin made of pearls, an empty gold locket, baby blankets. Also two blouses: a funereal black one, and a yellow one dotted with a flower motif pleasing to the eye. She had been a large woman. In their marriage portrait, Evangeline Dodds towered over her husband, Gilly, as Lucie Peloquin towered over Cyril.

The blouse fit just right, the arms only a little short above his wrists. Most importantly the buttons were intact. He could roll the sleeves. Putting his tattered vest back on over his new shirt, he went to the window again, hoping they would come out for recess, making their way down the steps just as he had once rushed out after Una, every recess. They had rarely spoken, but through the years he had watched her from various vantage points on the outskirts of the schoolyard, where he would not be noticed. He waited a while longer, but the Wisharts did not emerge. Since he had patched the walls, it was probably colder outside than indoors.

She came the following day as evening settled in. Abel stopped hammering the paddock gate — which Tansy had slipped through — and his mare raised her head from a tuft of hay as Una crossed the fields between their farmsteads, her lantern swaying above the ground like a fallen star.

Feeling the blood rush to his face, he fiddled with his tools as she neared him.

"Hello. I just..." She turned to blow her nose into an embroidered handkerchief. "I'd like us to start over."

She wore what looked like her brother's boots and coveralls under her coat, and a red toque, scarf and mittens knit from the same ribbed pattern. Tansy lowered her head over the gate. Una petted her muzzle. "Remember how she used to chase after Dukey? Remember how we raced for fun?"

This was not how Abel remembered it. Rather, Una's horse — a high-spirited beast called Marmaduke — used to charge after Tansy. On occasion, Una had challenged Abel to a sprint from the schoolyard hitching rail, leaving him and Tansy in the dust as she galloped past on her dark gelding.

She glanced around the barren property and beyond, toward Grayley. Their town that was no longer a town. Her lips, he thought, looked blue.

"Tea?" he offered.

"Oh, no. I..." she shivered. "Well, alright then. As the British say, a cup of tea cures everything."

Lowering her lamp's wick, she followed him to the house.

Hanging her scarf, toque and mittens, she kept her coat on as she walked around the living room, crouching here and there to read the newsprint on the walls. "These are sorely out of date."

"That d-doesn't change what's happened."

"Don't you think it's awful?" She straightened. "How the other countries aren't doing a thing, letting them... get away with this?"

"You mean the c-camps."

"I mean everything. All this hatred and bullying." She sat at the table. "I never understood why Hitler wasn't punished when he disregarded the Versailles treaty. He's a disgraceful human being."

"He's— turned Germany into a strong nation." Abel struggled with the teapot lid. "Their economy is b-booming. There's no depression or joblessness there."

Una gasped. "Are you forgetting the Nuremberg Laws? And Kristallnacht?"

"The Germans voted him in." The lid slid into place.

"Yes, then he turned their democracy into a dictatorship." She crossed her arms. "I see what you're doing, Abel Dodds. You're sparring on purpose. Like you used to do in school. I won't fall for it."

He sat across from her and poured their tea. He wished he had something sweet to offer. Instead he gave her his mother's porcelain cup, pink with hand-painted meadowlarks.

"These may feel like tough times." She stared into the cup. "But I think we'll look back on these days as good ones."

She glanced up at him. His breath caught then. How was it that she saw through everything, offering insight as minor passing comment?

She rose and approached his parents' wedding portrait on the radio cabinet.

The couple who stood before the camera on the open prairie were strangers to Abel. This version of his father in a well-fitted suit with a trimmed moustache, clasping his bride's hand. In her lace gown and swept-back veil, Evangeline stood a foot taller than her husband. Both younger than Abel was now, with open-mouthed smiles. They looked as if they were laughing. Normally couples in such portraits appeared stern. When Abel had asked his father what was so funny, Gilly Dodds replied, "We were just happy, son."

Una smiled at his parents and set down the frame.

Returning to the kitchen, she sat in the rocker. Closing her eyes, she rested her head against the chair's high back. "I wonder how George and Elizabeth feel about their upcoming travels. I'll bet they're nervous." She set the chair to rocking. "Seeing as George didn't even want the job of king. Now the poor man has to worry not only about managing his stutter, but also about his whole country being destroyed while he's stuck on a sightseeing tour." She opened her eyes and stared at the ceiling. "And the queen's got to trek halfway across the globe to be by his side, when most likely she just wants to stay home with her girls. Just thinking about all they'll have to do to pay us tribute tires me out. Putting on a brave face, no matter how they're feeling or how they'll be received." Pushing herself up, she returned to the table and pulled an envelope from her pocket. Another was stuck to it and fell to the ground. She picked it up, looking it over. "Brynn's new year wishes, late as usual. I suppose my sister writes when she can, between her studies. I should write more, too." She slipped it back into her pocket, showing Abel the other envelope addressed to Their Majesties King George VI and Queen Elizabeth. "I thought the tour could be a way to incorporate geography and arithmetic into his lessons. I hadn't anticipated..." She put a hand to her forehead. "It's Toby's official invitation. We haven't even got a stamp."

How many thousands of others were sending such letters, Abel wondered. And how long before it got picked up from the Royal Mail postbox at the station, which was emptied inconsistently, if at all.

He retrieved his father's sewing tin from the smoking table's interior compartment and gave her a stamp. A stamp with the king's face on it, just like their money. Wordlessly she licked and pressed it onto the envelope.

Her cheeks were flushed. He wanted to ask why she had not made something of herself, away from their insignificant town, when she'd had the chance. Why she had reappeared, unwed and saddled with a child, when she was so much better than a commonplace life in Grayley. It never made sense to him, that she had returned while both her siblings got away. He wanted to shout, *What were you thinking, coming back here?*

Wiping crumbs off the table, she sipped her tea. "Anyway. Why should the king and queen not come to our river of roses."

He forced a laugh. "What— river?" The river had long dried up. Only dust and dead roses remained. A rose dust river.

"Have you forgotten that day with Miss Kitty? The roses *are* the river." She waited but he had nothing to say. "Remember we went collecting blooms to study plant anatomy? That sunny day we sat by the water, and Miss Kitty told us it didn't matter where we came from. Or what we didn't have. She made us lie back, close our eyes and smell the perfume of those roses. She said the scent alone could keep us afloat through hardship. Remember?"

He would have. He would have remembered this with all his being. Only the excursion had probably occurred on one of those days he was out working the fields with his father, missing school. Una had forgotten that he had not been there.

"I remember," he said.

She moved to the window, looking out at the growing darkness. Somewhere a coyote called. "I've been thinking . . ." She turned back to him. "What if the king and queen's visit saves us from war? If Hitler sees how strongly united we are with Europe, and it frightens him off?"

This was the other side of Una. The side that had always frustrated Abel. She believed in fantastical notions. The stories Miss Kitty told, she had believed. He remembered her believing in King Arthur, and Avalon, and that whole preposterous sword-in-the-stone legend. Now here she was, a grown woman, still holding on to the same naive convictions she had as schoolgirl, that anything was possible.

Who was he to cast a pall over her latest whim? She would find out for herself.

She reached for her scarf. "We'll never share the same view of the royal family." She pulled her toque down over her ears and slipped her hands into her threadbare mittens.

He went to the counter for some bread. "Do you have enough—"

She shook her head. "We've got plenty."

He accompanied her outside, waiting as the glow from her lamp crossed the fields. He had no doubt that if a band of coyotes approached, she would convince them of the importance of the upcoming Royal Tour, and how it could save them all.

Walking to the stable, he rebuked himself for mulling over the war. It was a waste of time. He tried not to make noise opening the door. Elizabeth Moon was lying down, ruminating. Tansy moved around a little in her stall, shifting her weight from one leg to another to find comfort.

He kept dwelling on the potential for war. If it came to it, farms would be called upon to feed the country, and those fighting abroad. Yet his father would say that to assume all farmers should be exempt from joining up was cowardly. If only his father had not served, Abel would feel more confident about his own stance. If only he were here to talk things through.

Covering Tansy with a blanket, he returned to the house.

In the kitchen he prepared a meal of buttered bread and fried white apples. They were really turnips — one of the few vegetables easy to dig up and which lasted through winter. Then he walked around the living room just as Una had done, crouching to read the newsprint, stopping at an article on Mackenzie King's invitation to their majesties, recently pasted by the floor. He tore it off the wall and sat with it in the rocker, swearing aloud, until he remembered the stone in his pocket.

At the kitchen basin he scrubbed it until the pattern revealed itself as a feather. A fossilized feather from an altogether different place and time. Belonging to a creature he could not imagine. Millions of years old.

The lamp in your window
aglow like the nugget
of gold in a hand-dug well.
—A.D.

5

Winter is for remembering to sleep, his father always said. With less to do now, Abel recalled Gilly Dodds' weariness subsiding by the end of January each year. As his father rested inside between the growing seasons, he woke late, canned vegetables and made jellies. He invented songs to pass the time, and played cards and checkers with Abel. Stretching out on the sofa with his pipe until late into the night, he told chilling tales involving children who vanished in the fields, prairie witches, phantom cattle bandits and haunted homesteads. Abel could have listened to his father's stories forever.

Nowadays he rarely slept.

The small coal heater in his bedroom provided little warmth. His parents' room, which still held the washstand and dresser, was even colder. The wind shifted, finding new ways in. The bedrooms had gotten so drafty, their windows layered in glittering frost, that he questioned their usefulness. The flatiron helped to heat his bed, but he sometimes woke in the night with tiny granules of ice coating his blankets. Abel wondered if the Wisharts endured the same. Or if they had fuel for their heaters.

Instead of easing off as he had done at this time of the year with his father, for the past several mornings Abel rose early, setting out for the Wise Men in the half darkness with Tansy and a lantern. Once he reached the leaning grain elevators, he walked along the rails, collecting coal that had spilled from trains.

Like food, relief coal was available to everyone now. But it meant a trip into Sterling, and why go to the trouble and humiliation, when he could find fuel on the plains. He just needed to kick away the snow, which Tansy did naturally as she walked, while Abel crouched between the ties for pieces. At first his fingers bled from scraping rocks. But by the time his bag was full, he hardly felt a thing in his extremities.

On his way back to the farm, he combed the pastures in search of sun-dried dung. The snow cover wasn't thick. It was easy to spot Elizabeth Moon's flat mounds that had decomposed in the heat of summer, now hard and burnable. Adding these to the bag of coal, he went to the shed for his best tin bucket, which he set on the workbench. In it he mixed the chips and coal, saving a small portion at the bottom of the bag for himself. Afterwards he cleaned his hands in the snow. Then he crossed the fields to the schoolhouse and left the offering on the steps, returning home with his horse by sunup.

Though he was against her teachings in praise of the British royal family, he didn't want the Wisharts to freeze. Especially not that wretched boy of hers, looking so forlorn. Sometimes, watching them, he felt his chest would explode.

Abel wondered if Una was purposely ignoring what this Royal Tour was really about. Like Prime Minister Mackenzie King, their majesties were losing favour. They knew Canada didn't need them anymore. And like Mackenzie King, Una was not considering those still facing unemployment, with no food on their tables, let alone homes. Those facing debt and crop failures, displacement and

Winter, 1939

upheaval, and lack of government support. Abel thought that for Una the visit served as a diversion. From recent atrocities committed by Hitler, and the approach of war, and how hard life was. She didn't seem to mind about ulterior motives. Her avoidance of critical thinking irked Abel. Especially when Miss Kitty had warned them that to accept ideas without question was a dangerous habit, amounting to intellectual laziness.

He spent the morning in the shed, performing maintenance on the binder. Removing hardened wheat stalk residue from the machine, he cleaned the components of grime, first with a wire brush, then with a damp rag, careful to not use much water, to avoid further rusting. He realigned the belts and sharpened the cutting blades with a file. He had no grease to lubricate the moving parts, but used motor oil, obtained from Cy Peloquin in exchange for his father's pickling jars.

In the afternoon he tended to the animals.

His horse and dairy cow hadn't always gotten along. But since he had moved Elizabeth Moon to the stable—she was sociable, he didn't want her stuck in the barn alone—she and Tansy had settled into a peaceful coexistence.

Both were getting on in years. Their time would soon be over. The dip in Tansy's back, her drooping lips and loss of muscle mass were becoming obvious. As for Elizabeth Moon, this would be her last year for milking, the calf she gave birth to in the fall already sold, and the breeding bulls gone.

Once they were of no use for labour, or riding, or producing, a farmer butchered aging stock for what meat they might provide. Abel couldn't bring himself to thinking about this yet.

His cow barely reacted as he milked her then rubbed her loose skin. Not much bothered Elizabeth Moon. Her spots, his father once told him, were like fingerprints. No two Holsteins were alike. She chewed and sniffed, and bore no grudges. At times she licked Abel's hands with her large, rough tongue. It hurt, but he let her do it anyway.

He added a little of the fall harvest's grain that hadn't been worth cutting to their roughage. No matter what he fed them — even food off his own plate — they were skinny. A partition divided their stalls. They leaned their heads over their low doors like two girls talking to one another over the feed bunk, as if to say, *Is this it? Is this all he's giving us, after everything we've done for him?*

Neither one liked the cold. But he forced them out to exercise, to walk around the yard in order to avoid the doldrums. Brushing their coats by the chicken coop, he looked up in time to see the Wisharts nearing the schoolhouse. When Una reached the steps, she paused at the bucket he'd left. Toby picked it up, and they passed inside.

Leading Tansy and Elizabeth Moon around for a final lap, he glanced over his shoulder and saw her emerge onto the steps again. She raised her arm in greeting, and he walked into the yard's iron pump. It worked, but produced no water. He couldn't manage to wave back so turned away, taking his mare and Holstein to their quarters.

A short time later, he was organizing tools in the shed when he heard the faint, distant rumble of a vehicle.

He stepped outside and raised his binoculars. Even though he didn't need to look through the lenses to see his surroundings clearly, he wore these most days — he felt the thin leather strap dig into the back of his neck even when he wasn't wearing them — to feel closer to his father, whose fingers had smoothed the blackened brass. Gilly Dodds had even added a side clip to the strap, sparing Abel the need to remove his hat when putting on or removing the glasses.

Turning the roller he spotted Harold Nettles' Ford approaching. The only green thing in Cutland County, the car glided along the main road. This was the week Abel had been expecting him. The banker always made his rounds the last week of every month.

Pulling up by the barn and cutting the engine, he got out of his shining vehicle with his briefcase. Abel never understood why he carried that thing around. He had never once seen him open it.

Winter, 1939

"Dodds!" Abel was walking toward the house. "This won't take a minute." He caught up and extended a hand.

Abel shook it hard. He would not be intimidated.

Harold Nettles wore tailored clothing and two-tone oxfords. Had the man any sense, he wouldn't flaunt such fineries and would travel by truck, like his banker father before him. Or by way of the Bennett buggy. Had Harold any common sense, he would have worn galoshes.

Even his pudginess during these lean times felt wrong. But he wasn't a bad person, Abel supposed. He looked up at the sky. "It keeps — coming."

"What's that?"

"Snow. It's a good sign."

Harold held out his palm, studied what landed there, then brushed his glove. "Dry, though," he said. "You need the wet, heavy stuff."

Abel knew what he was thinking. How far the farm had fallen since Abel's father first rented the piece of land, until he had accumulated enough from two years of good crops to make a down payment. Grain prices were at an all-time high by the time Gilly Dodds purchased their new tractor, binder and threshing machine, all on credit. Like so many, his father bought and bought, without care about what would be owed on equipment and seed loans. On the mortgage, and property, and taxes.

Every year Abel tried to pay the interest on the debt. The rest he would pay when the rains came.

"You're in arrears again," the banker told him.

"G-give me till summer."

Harold Nettles scratched under his collar and looked around. Abel stayed by the house as Harold went into the stable and shed, then the barn and coop. He even walked a ways into the field, pulled a blade from his pocket, and picked at the frozen ground.

"I'll see what I can do," he said when he returned. "But you should think of selling. And finding other work." He put a hand on Abel's shoulder. "I don't want you forced out."

Debt was no reason to leave, in Abel's opinion. Everyone on the prairie was in debt, owing their farms and stock, dry fields and rusting equipment, automobiles, electricity and telephones, to the bank. Though most, he knew, had gone off to start again elsewhere, erasing past dues.

He had given everything up already—his whole life—for this place. "I just need— one more harvest."

Harold Nettles followed Abel's gaze across the field, to the schoolhouse. The afternoon session was over. Una, Toby and Merle filed out through the veil of snow. The banker bid Abel farewell, returned to his automobile, put his unopened briefcase back inside and drove off in the direction of the Wisharts.

If the snow kept up, the roads would soon be unpassable. Abel would be glad when collectors and repossession agents would be prevented from travel. When only the coyotes and the trains could get through.

After the banker's visit he went back to the shed to take stock of what would need replacing come spring, which bolts, bins, shovels and saws could no longer be fixed or reused. Counting nails, he could think of nothing but his family's debt, and his father.

He walked over to the barn, whose red paint had been eaten off by grasshoppers. It had stood empty since the cull. His father had been so proud of their small dairy. Though he was fairly certain Gilly Dodds would have done the same, Abel would always feel like a murderer.

Without cattle, the barn served as a storage space for hay and straw, and bags of grains and turnips. Broken-down equipment like plows and harrows. A museum of nests of swallows.

He rummaged around for planks to burn. Had his father not taken such delight in the structure he had singlehandedly built—he spent more nights in the barn than in the house — Abel would have long ago pulled it apart for fuel.

A mouse darted across the dirt floor, disappearing behind a pile of rope.

Abel sat on a milking stool.

They'd had their best talks here, wrapped in wool blankets, waiting for calves to be born. Once, Gilly had come in and found Abel sleeping, textbooks flung aside. He'd shaken him awake. "What's this?" He'd reached for the open notebook on a bale.

Abel grabbed the scribbler from him.

"Looks like a poem." His father struck a match and lit his pipe. "You writin' poetry, son?"

"It's nothing."

"You know, I was quite the raconteur in my day. That's how I wooed your mother. There's no shame in poetry."

Weeks later, Abel discovered a dog-eared book left on that same bale. Alfred, Lord Tennyson's *Idylls of the King*. His father had attended the implements fair in Sterling, and must have gotten it there. Likely depriving himself of a visit to the tobacco shop.

Abel had to look the word up. *Idyll*. He'd never heard it before. It meant an extremely wonderful period of time. A happy, pastoral interlude. A briefly lived scene.

The story was about the fall of King Arthur. But he didn't care much about the poem's romantic themes of chivalry. The idylls were blank verse — what Abel learned from Tennyson was that his own thoughts didn't need to rhyme.

He never acknowledged his father's gift. Nor did Gilly Dodds mention his poetry writing again. To this day Abel felt badly that he hadn't thanked him. For that and many other things. Like the afternoon Abel came home and announced he was quitting school, having made the decision after months idling around the schoolyard while his father struggled alone in the fields.

"No, you're not." His father dug at the soil.

"You need help running things. The farm'll soon be — worthless."

"Your mother would've disagreed that schooling's wasted time." He wiped his brow. "Besides, you like going?"

Sitting behind Una Maeve. Learning about the world from Miss Kitty. *Like* was not strong enough a word for how Abel felt some days, at the rushes of information his teacher threw at him, or at a glance Una aimed at him. He was mad about going. Completely mad and filled with adoration. He swallowed, nodding to his father.

"That settles it, then."

"But we've — got no money."

His father rested his boot on the spade. Although he was supposed to have turned in his uniform and equipment at discharge, Gilly Dodds had somehow managed to buy a few souvenirs to take home — namely his service boots, binoculars, canteen and the Lee-Enfield. He'd never repaired the hole in the top of the right boot. His big toe, black with bruising, poked through the sock and through the boot's shredded leather.

"Sure we've got money." Abel's father pointed at the ground. "We got all we need right here. Just hidden."

That hazy evening, they came in from the field and sat on the paddock fence as the blood-red sun went down, and Abel's father recounted his one and only war story.

The story concerned a fellow named Hoyt Sanderson from Orchardtown, Saskatchewan, known to everyone as Happy for his unabashed smile.

Happy missed his acreage. But like Abel's father, he was among those farmers who believed in individual sacrifice for the greater good, and enlisted willingly.

He had no loved ones or sweetheart. His longing was for the prairies — he missed bobolinks and snowdrifts and hockey, and spoke with fondness of threshing gangs, and evening primrose blooming in ditches. He missed his Labrador retriever and his free-roaming mustang, and campfires and tinned sardines.

After their lieutenant saw how good he was with animals, Happy was given the responsibility of tending to wounded horses that served their battalion, or shooting them, if their suffering was too great. Most were pack animals, not cavalry horses, and were animals not meant for battle. At times it seemed there were more horses than soldiers. Thousands upon thousands, needing to heal from artillery wounds, skin ailments, hoof infections and poison-gas injuries. So they could be returned to the front lines.

Wherever he went, Happy erected memorials for dead horses. Some assembled from sandbags and barbed wire. Others from shattered helmets and mess tins. Eventually he started sleeping in the improvised enclosures made from canvas sheets where the animals slept, and speaking less and less.

During the Somme offensive, Happy ran out of ammunition. Dropping his rifle, he sat by a black gelding, trying to soothe it with gentle strokes. For seven hours he did not leave the horse's side. Waiting out the gunfire—he kicked at his comrades who tried dragging him away—he stayed in the mud until the great gelding passed on.

Then the farmer from Orchardtown reached into the saddlebag and found a thin bar of gold. As if the beast were telling him, *Thank you.*

This unexpected gift sustained Happy for some time. Standing in mud for weeks, rats gnawing at his food supplies and tacks and harnesses, half-deaf from blasts of artillery fire, he smiled.

Happy Sanderson fell down a well as a boy, enduring a week in deep darkness, until rescue came. Happy whistled through rheumatic fever, and later survived a barn fire. Happy chewed on strands of straw and sang Christian songs while marching. Happy loved horses and wore that thin bar of gold against his chest with a wrapped bandage, and twice was struck with gunfire where the bar protected him, and was saved, and saved again.

But the horses could not be saved, and the enormity of this truth did him in.

Once the war was over, Happy Sanderson lay down in the battlefield too, sweating and shivering. Gilly Dodds tried helping him up—he had no apparent injuries. But Happy only said, "I'm finished with all this. Take my gold and may it protect you."

After the young man stopped breathing, Gilly unwrapped his companion's bandage and peeled the bullion off his skin, which was inflamed with lice bites and scabs, and dragged him to a mound where horses lay and poppies grew.

"I brought it home," Abel's father told him that evening on their drying cropland. "Hid that precious yellow under this here soil. For when we need saving."

Only, he died before telling Abel where to find the treasure.

After Gilly Dodds' passing, Abel tore up the fields, marking each spot he dug into with a fistful of small stones so he wouldn't dig there again. He reached inside hundreds of gopher holes. He looked down shuttered wells and along the track. He checked the Wise Men, and pulled up paddock posts.

Digging, then filling the holes back up and flattening the earth so that no creature would twist an ankle, Abel often thought about what was real versus what was imagined.

If one invented a legend and believed long and hard enough, could it be made true? He thought of King Arthur, fabled ruler who went wounded from the battlefield to heal in a wondrous place where fruit trees grew. He thought how in Arthur's realm, myths about gold-carrying animals, and war-ravaged lands where soldiers died but passed to a better state of being, were common. But mostly, as he made holes and filled them, Abel thought about his father. Because of him, he vowed he would not stop digging. In search of a buried idyll.

*Winter drapes garlands
of frost over you.
Quills of light in your hair.*
—A.D.

6

Not once, that day she'd come by, did Una complain about the gaps in the schoolhouse floorboards, through which an arctic cold seeped. Abel remembered the subpar heating from their time there, when pupils stomped their feet to keep warm, like a corral of half-frozen colts.

She didn't seem to care about being chilly, but she did bemoan their lack of composition books and writing instruments. She had a few pencils but was down to her last nub of chalk, and feared that Toby would not be impressed with the trays of sand and twigs she would resort to next for lessons.

He had finally got around to making chalks, mixing cornstarch with water in three bowls, stirring in drops from his parents' old colouring vials — yellow from the goldenrod and pink from the rosehip. The third bowl he left white, pouring the contents of the bowls into his father's candy mould, shaped like seashells, which he then set out to harden on the sill.

Now he tapped the chalks out, thinking, how senseless to have shells in an area as landlocked as the desert. Of all the shapes his father could have chosen. Then he thought, *Why am I wasting time on such frivolities?* They needed firewood. Soon there would be nothing left for the cookstoves. Even from afar, he could see the racks against the schoolhouse and Wishart house diminishing. Jake hadn't bartered for enough timber, or collected enough of the summer's woody shrubs.

He decided on the collapsed, dust-filled privy, situated away from the farmhouse down a narrow, worn trail. After building a more solid structure, Gilly Dodds had left it standing for sentimental reasons. He had carved the coat hooks himself, and the candle shelf adorned with vines. He called it their sentry box.

With a claw hammer and crowbar, Abel pulled apart the salvageable planks, including one with a cut-out heart window. Sawing and stacking a good amount of wood into the old buckboard, he gave himself slivers he barely felt go through his stiff fingers. After he finished, he swept up loose shavings, adding these to the pouch of Tansy's hair he had been gathering every time he groomed her.

He had an idea to keep the schoolhouse warm from the middle of the room, so that the heat could radiate more evenly.

Hauling an oil drum out of the shed, he drove a nail through the bottom and sides, making holes to let oxygen in, to lessen smoke. Cutting some coop wire into a grated lid for sparks, he loaded these with a sack of sand into the wagon. From the positioning of the sun behind a slab of cloud, he guessed it was shy of noon. Strapping the cart to Tansy, he helped her pull it across the field, knowing the Wisharts would not yet be there.

Once they reached the schoolhouse, he covered his mare with a blanket and toted in the supplies. Rolling the burn barrel into the middle of the room he spread sand beneath it, filled it with wood and kindled the fire, rearranging the apple crate seats and desks so that they were near the barrel.

Laying out the chalks, waiting for the space to warm, he looked

Winter, 1939

around and found the classroom changed. Over the past few weeks the Wisharts had been busy.

They had drawn a map of the Royal Tour route in pencil on tea towels stitched together. Tacked up, the map covered a good deal of the king's grubby wall.

In loopy handwriting across the top, someone had written *The Royal Visit to Canada in May, 1939*. On the map were sketched triangles for trees and mountains, grassy lines for plains, waves for bodies of water, canoes for ferry crossings and Vs for birds. Houses for cities and stick people for populations.

Standing in front of the map, Abel followed the route of all the places the king and queen would see: every province, the Dominion of Newfoundland, and a little of the United States. The Royal Train would steam west along the Canadian Pacific track, returning all the way to the Maritimes on the Canadian National track. The railway lines connecting the country's towns and cities were illustrated with one line which read *CP—Going*, and another which read *CNR—Returning*.

Official stops were also written out: *Wolfe's Cove* in *Quebec City. Ottawa. Regina. Calgary. Victoria. New York City. Saint John. Charlottetown.* The small, unimportant town of Grayley, Alberta, was marked along the rail line with a single rosehip.

Wood crackled in the burn barrel but the room still felt cold. Abel sought out crevices between the wall planks and lost track of time doing patchwork—he had made a paste with the wood shavings from the privy, and Tansy's hair, mixing these with glue he found in the utility cupboard, and it seemed to be working—when he heard them coming.

"Did the king and queen go to the same school?" the boy asked from the cloakroom between fits of coughing. "Is that how they met?"

"I'm not sure of the circumstances," his mother said. "But I can tell you that Lady Elizabeth turned down the prince's first proposals."

"On account of his stammer?"

"I don't think the way he spoke bothered her. I think it was more that... she wanted to retain her independence. Oh! Hello." Una stepped back from where Abel knelt by the clock with his putty knife, while Toby and Merle went straight to the barrel.

"Golly." Sparks rose into the air. "That is some fire. We've been meaning to thank you for the coal," she added. "Your mix gives off good heat."

Merle lit his pipe, wheezing as he breathed in. "And it's not smelly."

Abel stood and nodded.

"Anyway," said Una, rejoining her family, "it turned out fine, because George and Elizabeth happened to be in love. Eventually she said yes and they became duke and duchess. Then came the princesses Elizabeth and Margaret."

Toby peered into the fire. "Then his brother had a romance."

"Yes, well. Edward was a charismatic fellow." She held her hands over the grate. "Prince Albert became King George, and took his brother's place, fulfilling his duty. He put his country above his personal desires."

"His application," Toby sniffed, "got him kicked out of the castle."

"Abdication." Una went to the board, discovered the new chalks, and glanced at Abel before spelling out the word. "He abdicated the throne two years ago, and left England."

"Was George sore at his brother"—her son chewed on a fingernail—"for making him be king?"

Una directed her words to the portrait on the wall. "He wasn't trained to be a monarch. It's probably been difficult for him. He's not a people person, I wouldn't say."

Toby pressed on. "Does the queen like people?"

"Yes. I think Elizabeth is opposite to the king in that way. As a young girl, for example, during the Great War, she even helped wounded soldiers when her home was made into a hospital." She approached the window, rubbing her arms. "But I don't think it's that the king dislikes people. He and the queen work hard in different ways."

"Work hard at— what, exactly?" Abel knelt again to patch.

"At pleasing everybody, for one." Una turned abruptly. "And that's not always easy."

She went outside to raise the flag. When she came back in they sang "God Save the King."

Why, thought Abel, did God have to be a part of everything? It was hypocritical having children sing a legislation song when the school board hadn't been bothered to provide adequate heat or supplies for years.

It had been a long time since Abel had believed in God. He believed in a sort of providence, maybe. A divine guidance which he saw simply as light. But not God.

Una had Toby practise his spelling by way of words from the legend of King Arthur. The boy stuck his tongue out in concentration, writing with his chalk shell on the board.

"You've forgotten a letter." She pointed at *Nights of the Round Table*. "You have it written as if nighttime were at the table. *Knight* the man has that silent letter we talked about. Like *knave*."

Toby stepped back, tilting his head up to Miss Kitty's alphabet along the top of the board. Then he added his *K*.

She quizzed him on the name of the knight's medieval court. After careful consideration he wrote, *Kamelot*.

"Close. But this one has no *K*. Remember your soft and hard *C*'s?"

Erasing the *K* he replaced it with a *C*. Then he wrote *Lancelot*, *Guinevere* and *Galahad*. *Excalibur*, *gauntlet* and *armour*. Eventually he put down his chalk and wandered back to the fire, teeth chattering. Stoking the flames with a twig, his brow furrowed. "Did King Arthur even exist?" He started to cough again.

"Just because there is no proof," Una rubbed his back, "doesn't mean he wasn't real. It's possible he was based on a historical military leader."

"A l-leader who was defeated," Abel said.

"He did his best, though." Una raised her chin a fraction. "To protect his country. He stayed loyal to his queen. No matter if she wasn't...worthy."

"The real hero," Merle offered, "was the wizard."

Toby rushed back to the board, spelling out *Merlin* as the sound of horse harness bells approached.

Abel wiped his putty knife and went to the window. The Peloquins rode up in their snowplane, a small wood hut with benches and a stove inside, pulled on skis by horses.

Cy Peloquin called "Hé!" and "Hou!" until his horses stopped next to the schoolhouse. Alighting from his seat behind the great brown geldings, he opened the hut door and his wife, Lucie, and seven of their nine children emerged from within, like a family of bright larks.

Merle welcomed them inside, squeezing Cyril's shoulder. Cy slapped his back and then Abel's. Then the whole family spilled in, everyone hugging and asking after each other.

Winters always felt long without the Peloquins, who left during the cold months, first to hunt, then passing back though Grayley only briefly on their way to stay with Cy's sisters further north. They used to have a farm as well. Their land was seized by the bank five years back, along with their pigs and cows, because they could not pay taxes. Instead of taking up on a vacant homestead from which they might again be forcibly removed, the family settled in one of the abandoned railcars scattered at intervals beside the line. These had once been used as shelters by workers making repairs on a stretch of railroad. On that track of Crown land, Cy claimed, the soil was no worse than anywhere else.

Once, over tea, Abel had asked Lucie about her family. To which Lucie replied, "I don't know who I am anymore. Too much of me was stolen. But no one bothers us here."

After their eviction, the Peloquin children were no longer

permitted to attend school. This did not deter Lucie, who taught them herself. The older ones helped the young ones learn. The Peloquin children were cleverer than many of Cutland County's pupils, who often missed half a year of lessons due to harvests, remoteness and winter roads. Even if the right foot did not always match the left, the Peloquins all had shoes. A skilled seamstress, Lucie made their clothing from flour sacks, fitting her family with shirts, pants and dresses marked with bleached out company names.

In '35 their two eldest sons, now working in the mines, had partaken in the On-to-Ottawa Trek and the Regina Riot, protesting relief camps and twenty-cent-a-day pay. The convoy never made it to the nation's capital. R.B. Bennett made sure to halt the freight train—with thousands of men sitting in seats and on the floor, and clinging to the roofs of the cars when there was no room left inside—by the time it reached Regina. But Cy Peloquin was still proud of his sons. "My boys took our damnable government to task," he liked to say.

Lucie was a formidable woman, as tall and stately as Cy was short and round. On their tiny piece of land, she had carved out a food cellar, and had the only garden in the area still producing bounteous vegetables. Gourds and cabbages. Yams, carrots and onions. She offered whatever she had extra to those worse off than herself—drifters, and people who lived in tarpaper shacks and sod huts in the miles east and west of Grayley. She never turned away anyone who arrived at the caboose. While Cy was off snaring and setting up hidden stills for hooch that he would sell to drinking establishments in the city, she foraged for berries and herbs, always knowing where to look for medicines that quelled all kinds of pain.

She slipped three pairs of hide mitts to the Wisharts while her husband approached the drum, offering his flask around.

"No big game this year," Cy said. "Only 'yotes." He scrutinized the blackboard. "R'garde-moi donc ça." He scratched his beard. "You know this here's a French tale. Best parts all writ by

Bretons. La table ronde. La liaison entr' Lancelot du Lac puis la reine Guenièvre. Le graal. Hein, chérie? The English stole it from us. Like they steal everything."

"Ça se peut," Lucie told her husband. "But a hero is still a hero. No matter where he's from." She had not taken her eyes off her children, who rushed around the drum, giggling, almost tipping it over. She cupped her hands into a thunderous clap "Dehors!" Her children ran outside, and Toby followed.

Cy lit his pipe. "Bon ben. The reason we stopped here."

Lucie sighed. "Cyril. Must you."

"Eh oui. I must." Bit between his teeth, he turned to Una. "Ma fille, we've known each other a long time. Dis-moi. What's this tittle-tattle—this ragot—Toby told our little'uns yesterday as we got home, and found your boy by the rails, collecting twigs?"

Una went to the bookshelf and returned with a mildewy book, dropping the clump of pulp in his lap. "In the absence of books, I thought the tour would make for an interesting lesson. That's all."

Cy tossed the book aside. "No one wants 'em coming."

"We want them coming." Una turned to her grandfather. "Tell him."

"Seems harmless enough."

"Crisse." Cy shook his head. "You people."

"Calme-toi." Lucie reached out, brushing dirt from her husband's coat.

He went to the window and watched his children playing, their laughter carrying into the cold room. "We're not under British rule anymore. Why bow down?" He returned to the drum.

"She means no offence, Frenchie." Merle handed Cy his flask.

"My father was tricked into coming here," Cy's face reddened, "'cause the government said they needed more farmers. We had to learn your language. Your culture. You didn't have to learn mine." He emptied his pipe into the fire, as if not realizing he had just lit it. "Schoolkids threw rocks at me. Once, the schoolmistress pulled me outside by the ear for talking French. Years before the crisse de

Règlement 17. When my sister brought me home and told maman what happened, she marched me back there and sat me back down at my desk, telling the teacher, 'C'est notre droit. Laissez-le tranquil pour l'amour de Dieu.' Soon as she left, rocks again. After that maman walked through town singing in French, talking only French to shopkeepers. We stopped going to church. Sometimes our father came home with a black eye or split lip. Our house got covered in dung. But maman persevered, even wrote letters to ministers. Till she got tired and died."

"It was pneumonia," Lucie whispered.

"It was anti-French sentiments that killed her. J'te jure." Cy kicked a crate. "They told us to come here. And I stayed on parce que Dieu m'a emmené cet ange là." He gazed at his wife. "But maman died because the imperial mother country loathed us."

Merle set his cowboy hat on his knee. "Come now, Cy."

"You're blaming the wrong people." Lucie put a hand on her husband's arm. "King George isn't responsible for this government's actions."

"The English are coming to subjugate us. Just like they did in their conquest of New France." He circled the drum. "My loyalty is to Canada. If l'Empire goes to war again and we're forced in by conscription, there will be a revolt. J'te le promets."

"That's a separate matter," Lucie said.

"Non, ma chère," he told her. "It isn't."

Una wrung her hands. Abel almost felt sorry for her.

She went over to the map and looked at Grayley. "The whole country will be following this journey. Just because we're out here, why should we be forgotten?" She turned back to them. "I'm tired of feeling beaten. We need something to look forward to."

"I think what Una is proposing," Lucie told her husband, "is that we make this a cheerful occasion." She nudged him. "You can play your fiddle."

When Cy looked into his wife's eyes his face softened. "On n'est même pas sûr de c'te maudit itinéraire."

"They're the king and queen," Lucie told him. "It's up to them where they stop. I hardly think they'll be told no if they want to get off here."

"What about the prime minister?" Cy crossed his arms at Una. "Are we to welcome that bastard too? He's never been further than Toronto. Never done a damn thing for us." He rolled his cap in his hands. "Maybe I'll make a tear bomb. Make 'em cry a little."

"La paix, Cyril," his wife said. "Pas la guerre."

The children ran back in then, filling the schoolhouse with mirthful noise, climbing all over their parents.

Cy and Lucie bickered, Cy pulled his wife close, kissing her as she laughed and pushed him away. Abel imagined what it would be like to have his own family. To live in a home brimming with life.

They stayed a while longer, sharing molasses sandwiches until Lucie said it was time to go. They had to reach Cy's sisters in Beaumont by week's end.

They all went out together.

While the Wisharts talked with Lucie, Abel and Cy fed the geldings. "Have you — got kerosene?"

"Ben sûr I got some."

"I'll — give you my bedroom stove for it. Come spring."

They shook on the trade. Cy unloaded a small barrel of kerosene from the snowplane, and gave Abel a fresh supply of peppermints.

"What do you think," Abel helped himself to hay from his friend's bag, "of Una's — idea?"

"I think we all got different ways of surviving." Cy sipped from his flask. "This visit's all about Hitler. It's government plotting."

"We c-c-could get their attention. When they come."

"Osti." Cy chuckled. "How so? Derail the train?"

Abel didn't know, exactly, what he wanted to do. Show the monarchs the reality of the depression. Make Mackenzie King pay. There were all sorts of ways to get a truth across.

Everyone said their goodbyes.

Winter, 1939

The Wisharts walked home. Lucie joined her husband on the seat behind the horses and the Peloqins left for Cy's sisters up north, with their children tucked inside the snowplane.

Abel remained at the edge of the schoolyard and looked west down the rail line, to town and the grain elevators. From where he stood the three pale grey structures looked like a castle with a great middle tower and a turret on each side. Surrounded by sky and moated by a dusting of snow with rifts of blue in it, reflected from above.

*Let us stay close as the wolf
swallows the last slip
of sun and lopes through
snow, digging graves.*
—A.D.

7

Over the next fortnight the Red Ensign remained lowered outside the schoolhouse. No one took it in. It flapped near the ground, bright as a soldier's scarlet tunic, and still nobody approached from the distant farm, the days too cold for learning.

Abel cleaned the stalls and spent time with Elizabeth Moon and Tansy, padding their bedding, trying to keep them warm with extra hay and blankets. He spoke words of encouragement to the hens, who barely clucked or squawked, huddled together for heat. He cleared out broken wagon wheels from the shed and chopped them up for wood, which he delivered to the Wishart house at morning twilight, when stars dressed the sky like a spray of pellets. And each day he leaned against the barn door and looked out at the station, waiting for something he could not name.

At night he dreamt she came to him.

He was on his hands and knees, digging in the dirt. What are you searching for? She asked, then knelt and dug next to him. They hit a pool of water. Rust-tinted water they drank and bathed in. Then he saw a train coming. Una vanished. The train derailed and a swirl of grit blew his farmhouse away, and Abel found himself in the pasture, surrounded by his father's dead dairy cows.

He was out securing loose posts around the paddock, cursing the wind, when he heard her. She was running toward him, calling out, just as she had in his dream. Something was wrong.

"It's Toby." She struggled through the snow. It wasn't deep — maybe half a foot — but she stumbled. "He can't breathe. I tried Lucie's medicines and compresses. I tried everything. We need a doctor."

Abel set aside his mallet. Neither of their farms had a functioning telephone anymore, or a working truck. The telegraph office and line at the station had also been cut.

"Grandad wants to ride out," she pulled off her toque, wiping her forehead, "but I think it's better... you'd get there quicker, I think."

The waxen sun rose slow and steady. It would be at least five hours to Sterling. The doctor wouldn't travel at night. Abel would have to leave now if he was to return before darkness set in.

"Someone will— need to milk Elizabeth Moon."

Una nodded and ran home.

Back in the house he put long underwear on beneath his pants, changed into dry wool socks, and wrapped rags and scarves around his neck and under his sweater. He put on his coat and boots, and gloves that Lucie had given him, along with a fur hat. Filling his father's canteen with water, he packed bullets, matches and bread, and a small sack of feed into a burlap bag. Then he strapped his snowshoes and rifle across his back and wet the coal in the stove.

Tansy was sleep-standing in the stable. She huffed when he approached and woke her. "The boy who p-pets and talks to you is ill." He ran his hands along her neck and shoulders before placing a blanket on her back. "We need to— get help."

She lowered her head and ate a little hay. He tacked her up while Elizabeth Moon let out a quavering moo. Leading Tansy from her stall, Abel rested his hand on the warm white strip between his cow's brown eyes. "We won't be long," he told her.

He pulled the door shut and climbed into the saddle. They set off in the direction of Sterling. His mare couldn't gallop anymore. But once they left Grayley behind, Tansy's walk turned into a trot. At the start of winter, he had removed her horseshoes to keep the snow from balling up in her hooves. So long as ice or crusted snow didn't cut her legs, she could manage. She didn't balk, though they moved against the wind.

He tried not to think about Una's distress or Toby's. How many of Cutland County's children had caught diseases brought on by dust and malnutrition? Each year illnesses came out of nowhere, spreading through prairie towns.

They passed farms of friends: the Tanakas who had ventured to the West Coast to take up fishing. The Ekharts who decided to try their luck in Calgary. The Zhuks who believed Manitoba would be better. And finally the Hoffmans, who just vanished, no one knew to where.

Along the rail line, clusters of tarpaper dwellings had cropped up since he had last passed by. Time was short, but someone here might be in trouble. Abel rode to each site to check, but over and over again, he and Tansy were greeted with a resounding silence.

The snow they travelled through was powdery for the most part. Tansy didn't have to work too hard. They had to go slowly so she wouldn't break into a sweat, which would be dangerous in this weather. But she had endurance and knew the way.

He let his mind wander.

What news would Harold Nettles bring the next time he came? Would the bank defer payment until harvest? Abel couldn't take out any more loans. Harold had been firm on that. If the bank refused his extension, the only way to keep the farm would be through a guarantor. Who was there left to ask? No one but the Wisharts, who were in the same position. If harvest covered expenses for the coming year, it would be alright. But this hadn't happened since

'29. If crops failed again, what choices remained? He could sell for a pittance at auction, though it was possible no buyer would come forward. Then the bank would buy his farm, offering the bare minimum.

What would he do after that? Work as a hand in someone else's fields? Head for the assembly line or take a job in Sterling? Abel hated the city. Hated the thought of going there even now. For him cities represented the corrupt practices of officials. Noisy centres of power where decisions were made by the wealthy few, affecting those on the fringe. Decisions made by those who knew nothing about reality.

He had to find his father's gold or he would wind up a hobo.

Maybe he should have gone to Albion Ranch with Jake Wishart after all. Jake seemed to have won at the game of life, coming home each spring with ample earnings. Jake loved crowds and card games and being entertained. Jake loved spending time with women.

It was Jake who had taken Abel to Sterling for what he called a lesson years ago. To learn something, Jake had said, that could not be gleaned from books. As the cold wind intensified and Tansy pinned her ears back in concentration, Abel felt his face grow hot at the thought of what transpired that fall Una had gone away.

Jake had just come home. He'd made money travelling with a threshing crew, going from farm to farm, working long hours all summer while Abel stayed behind to be near his father, who was by then confined to the sanatorium.

One evening soon after his return, Jake and his chums threw a paper bag over Abel's head, roped his wrists behind his back, and pushed him into a car with exuberant shouts. An initiation of sorts. They drove to the city, to a place called Jubilee House, where they removed the bag.

Situated above a jazz club, Jubilee House was filled with men and women who seemed always to be celebrating. At Jubilee House a gramophone played and drinks were poured. As the longcase clock struck the hour, girls in sequined dresses led men down narrow hallways to private rooms.

Abel wasn't stupid. He knew Jake had brought him to a house of ill repute. While his captors mingled with the girls, he stood in the corner studying drapes the colour of wine. In the room were velvet club chairs and elegant mahogany furniture. Candles emitting a soft glow, dripping wax into silver holders on tables. Ferns unfurling on pedestals—Abel wondered how the plants survived with the smoke—and a gilded mirror so large he recoiled at the sight of himself.

Before that mirror Jake introduced him to Lorelei Schlegel from Stuttgart, Germany. Lorelei of the blond locks and pink lips, who wore a chiffon dress reaching just to the knee, and a feathered headpiece the same blue as her eyes.

Lorelei led Abel to a room lit by sconces. They sat together on the settee. An ivory comb and brush set rested on the dresser, and Abel wondered if he should smooth his hair, or fold and put away his clothing. Unsure of what to discuss, he enquired why her parents had named her after the maiden who lured fishermen to their deaths with her singing. Lorelei said she could neither sing nor swim. How did he know the myth anyway, she asked, putting her cigarette holder to his lips. He explained that he had finished his schooling, and knew his mythology, and was going to go on to university. Until his father became ill.

She shushed him and led him onto the bed of satin sheets.

When Abel was with Lorelei he didn't stutter. She never commented on his scarred cheeks. An hour into the liaison, lost in her murmurings, he convinced himself that this was a true, and profound, affection.

What was Jubilee House? A time of bliss. A place to be set free.

He came back again to the brothel on his own. After his father was gone, and harvests shrivelled up. After Una returned to Grayley with her boy.

He sold the graduation cufflinks his father had given him, his favourite pocketknife, and sets of tools, to pay the fee. Until one night when he appeared at the oak doors, and the woman in lace who let men in—a matronly figure with a hook of gleaming keys—said that Lorelei had gone back to Germany. To marry a military captain. And Abel realized how weak-minded he had been. To carry on this arrangement with someone pretending to feel for him, for a paltry sum.

Tansy skittered. He calmed her, stroking her neck and withers, and they kept going.

He thought about the news he'd heard the other evening—he couldn't get the report out of his head. A gathering in New York City, of all places! A pro-American rally at Madison Square Garden, where more than twenty thousand people assembled to cheer on the Nazi regime, with permission from local authorities. Would such heinousness next be authorized in Canada?

Tansy took fright again and reared, nearly throwing him. From the corner of his eye came a movement. A wolf, about ten yards off. Twice as big as a coyote.

If the animal was hungry or if a pack hunted nearby, they could close in from all directions. No matter her size Tansy was prey. A few nips to her legs would be disastrous.

Reaching for his rifle and loading, he stared the animal down until it turned, taking distance. He and his mare carried on. But the wolf continued at their periphery. Maybe it was just a nuisance, not a real danger, as wolves often were. If that was the case, why waste a bullet, or shoot a spook.

Abel's face grew cold. Frost formed on his eyebrows and eyelashes. How long had they been travelling? At least three hours, he estimated.

They were more than halfway there when they reached a desolate ranch with a bed of livestock bones. What had gone wrong with this culling, that the remains had not been disposed of properly? Abel called out hello, but there were no sounds of animals, machinery or humans. The calm was eerie. The barn warped at odd angles, distorted by weather. The stock pens were flattened, the fencing askew as if a herd had trampled through, fleeing as far as the pasture. The house's front windows were smashed and the door lay flat on the porch. Without dismounting Abel peered through a broken window to the kitchen. The table was set with four plates, a jar of desiccated yarrow and a lone chair. Ready for a person to dine with the departed. The odour of decaying animal remains hung in the air. Abel felt the hair rising from his arms, and they rode away.

From then on it was slow going with Tansy, who shortened her stride and turned her head from side to side, alert.

Working at his speech to keep his lips warm, Abel wondered if King George ever did such exercises. Repeating multi-syllable words with consonant sounds, as Miss Kitty had shown him to do. Speaking in slow motion, avoiding the urge to force out phrases too quickly.

Toby must be very sick. For Una to ask for the doctor.

Abel hated doctors as much as he hated going to the city. A doctor sent his father away, that spring he started coughing and spitting blood. A young, transient doctor, putting in his time before moving to a practice in a bigger hub. Abel couldn't recall the name of this fellow who came to examine Gilly Dodds and who arranged for X-rays. But he remembered the doctor's dismay, glancing around the farm as he lectured Abel on the importance of hygiene. Judging them by their poverty. A week later he returned to say it was tuberculosis. The poor man's disease. Telling him that his father must go to the sanatorium, and that the government would take care of the cost.

His father signed consent forms for Abel to stay on at the farm without a guardian, as he was only seventeen. Within hours the medical bus was at their door. Abel thought it unnecessary to remove him so swiftly, giving them no time together after the news. What difference would a day or two have made? His father pleaded to the men in white as they led him out, that he wanted to finish his crossword, and say goodbye to his son. But they wouldn't let him take any belongings, or hug Abel.

In the Cutland County Convalescence Home — a large stone building in the middle of a stark field — Gilly Dodds lay in a high-ceilinged hall filled with rows of hospital beds. At first Abel wasn't allowed to visit. He heard rumours that patients were forced to keep still all day, except if they needed to use the facilities. They weren't allowed to walk or bathe, and they were told not to breathe deeply. Nor could they listen to the radio or read newspapers, since any emotional response — including laughter — might lead to physical strain.

When Abel was finally granted access, after weeks of being turned away, he snuck in currants and rosehip jelly.

He was permitted monthly visits. During each one he wheeled his father out to the porch for fresh air. "Win that money and go to school," Gilly Dodds told him. "Forget the hard life here." It was June, toward the end of his last term. Of course there was no question of Abel going off to university. Nor did he want to anymore. In the end he told him that he had tried, but lost the scholarship to Una Wishart. His father then said, "Never you mind, son. Read me an idyll."

From the porch of the sanatorium they could see Horseshoe River.

Patients were wheeled out, even in bitter cold, as part of their treatment. The cold air and sunlight were believed to reduce the risk of infections, and help heal the lungs. Along with the others lined up along the porch, they witnessed the water flow, ripple and freeze over. A year passed in this way, with Abel working the farm and visiting his father, who drifted in and out of consciousness. When he slept, his arms moved through the air as if he were swimming. Each visit, Abel brought him a stone from the Horseshoe. Gilly's bed was near the window. First he had three stones, then six on the sill. Every stone marked a month. Some contained orange stripes and others were a deep purple hue. Still others held glassy bits.

Then the river dried and the stones in the riverbed turned grey.

His father was examined and re-examined, and Abel was told he wasn't healing as he should be. He was in respiratory distress. They removed some ribs and collapsed one of his lungs. His shoulders became uneven. Often he cried out in pain. When Abel helped him get up from bed to use the facilities, he could see his father had become humpbacked.

His cough and fevers worsened. It surprised Abel when the stones reached ten, then twelve. After that he lost count. One day Abel awoke from his chair next to the bed and saw the sun on his father's face, the doctor standing beside him, and the priest.

"Gather your strength and come home," the priest said, and Gilly Dodds was gone.

Abel collected his father's stones and set them in a circle around his parents' headstones in the cemetery. They were all he could offer in the way of memorial.

While ill, his father had consulted a legal professional. Abel inherited the farm, and all outstanding debts became his own. Every day that spring he walked the ice-laden bed of the Horseshoe River, until the ground thawed. But the river had evaporated from the land. No water had flowed there since.

The wolf followed at a distance. Tansy kept focused until the wind picked up and walloped them. The countryside darkened, a blackout curtain pulled over the sky. Snow and grit whipped them, blowing in all directions. The blizzard contained years of dust. The kind of weather in which one tied a rope from the house to the barn for guidance, or dug oneself into haystacks when stranded in a field.

Tansy turned sideways and wouldn't advance.

The wolf crossed their path, whimpered and barked, and ran

in bursts toward a structure of blurred contours, which appeared and disappeared in the blinding squall. Tansy whinnied. Abel dismounted and took her reins. He lowered his head and forged on, pushing through the wall of ice-sand coming at them. Each step threatened to pull them down. He lost a boot and had to backtrack as Tansy struggled to free herself. In the baleful wind the ice-sand was like a mass of clinging burs. He hated to think of Tansy's anxiety as he removed the accumulation—sticking inside her ears and nostrils, coating her mouth—before she suffocated.

The shelter he found was a barn near the point of collapsing. It whistled and creaked. Some beams had already given way, but what choice was there? He forced open the door, coaxing his mare forward with the promise of an apple.

As soon as they were inside Tansy snorted and roared. It sounded to Abel like a human scream. He struggled to hold her steady, looking around for the source of her distress. He lit a match and illuminated the carcass of a horse, its frozen foal curled up beside it. Torn open, the organs picked clean.

He turned Tansy away from the bodies. "I'm sorry this is un-unpleasant," he told her. "But we have— to wait it out."

Abel drank from his canteen, and then he poured what remained into the gallon bucket he'd tied to the saddle. Tansy had exerted herself too much. Her coat was sweaty and he'd have to keep her warm until it dried. Turning his hide gloves inside out, he brushed her. Then he fed her oats and grains from the sack, leaving the barn door open a crack so she could focus on the hypnotizing storm that enveloped them.

He once had found such storms terrifying. Now he watched, listened and waited.

In a corner, a brittle pile of mouldy hay released clouds of dust when he gathered some to cover the bodies. What horror had occurred here? No one in their right mind would abandon two healthy animals. But then, these past years many people had lost their minds. This was not a farm he knew, and he couldn't tell whether the attack had come from man or beast. Even the horses' eyes were gone. The tongues and tails. But their coats still shone, preserved by the cold.

He walked the perimeter of the barn, looking for material to burn, stepping on planks to loosen, crack and split them. Why had he not brought his axe! Because it was stuck in the field. It took twice as long as it would have otherwise, to gather enough wood.

Abel decided that Tansy wouldn't scare if he warned her in advance. "I'm going to m-make a fire. Nothing to be— afraid of."

Forming a small pyramid on the dirt floor, he lit a match. His shaking hands extinguished it before he could set it under the pieces of firewood. He lit a second match, then a third, covering his mouth with the collar of his coat to still his numb lips enough to blow, until a flame took hold and the wood smoked and burned.

He tried not to worry about Toby. Children were resilient. One day he wouldn't remember this. Only Abel would remember, and Una, whose state of distress was what most agonized him.

The fire began to warm them. The storm raged on and the barn swayed. He pushed the door open a little more to look for the wolf, but it was nowhere to be seen in the tempest. Not wanting to lie down in case a quick exit was needed, Abel leaned on his horse, closed his eyes and thought of Una.

His desk behind hers. Miss Kitty cheering both of them on. *My two bright stars*, she had once whispered to them. The odd time Una turned to chat with him, he'd catch whiffs of rosewater perfume. And Miss Kitty would say, "Una Maeve, quit flirting and keep focused." Abel knew Miss Kitty teased him out of kindness. Just as he knew Una felt nothing for him. But he was the only one who could compete with her intelligence. "I won't be bound or tied," he once heard her tell their teacher, "I won't be tapestry." She was smart enough to go anywhere.

Once, he snipped a lock of her hair with his pocketknife as it brushed across his desk.

He stood apart, by the track, while she played games in the

schoolyard. Sometimes she would approach him and ask him questions, searching the sky as if in deep reflection. "Abel, what do you think of such and such?" Or she would tell the others, "Oh, I don't know. Ask Abel, he's the smart one."

Only one of them could win the scholarship. Abel made no effort during exams. He thought, *She is too good for this place. She should be the one to go.* Even if his father hadn't become ill, it was what he would have done.

And she had left. For a time.

In his daydreams, Lorelei Schlegel and all logic aside, he had imagined that one day he might join Una. Until she showed up on the train platform a year and a half later with a baby, becoming tapestry. This was what Abel could not forgive. That Una had had her chance — one chance for them both — and she had tossed it down a well.

And now the world was on the brink of another abysmal war.

Tansy nickered and he came to, straightening himself at her side. The fire had died. Outside, the storm was subsiding. Adjusting the saddle, he pushed the barn door open and got on his horse, glancing back as the structure howled in the wind.

Sparks glowed in the ashes by the horses' bodies. *Let it catch fire*, he thought, and they moved away.

Tansy walked slowly, avoiding snowdrifts and ice patches. The wind eased off. How often had apocalyptic weather occurred this past decade, arriving out of nowhere, wreaking havoc? Then silence. The sky dissolving to cornflower-blue.

They rode for an hour, and another.

A plow train passed on the rail line, ahead of a freighter. They were nearly there. One more great boulder to pass. One more grain elevator to go.

Then the wolf reappeared and ran toward them. Abel hadn't seen it till then — it was as though it had emerged from a trap door under the new snow, loping over the landscape, kicking up grit and white. Coming toward them, teeth bared, tongue lolling.

Winter, 1939

Tansy braced her neck upward. Her eyes widened and her nostrils flared.

Abel reached for his rifle and fired.

Calming his horse, he dismounted and approached the animal. The wolf's golden eye locked on him as if in recognition. As if to say, *I only wanted to say hello.*

A half hour later they reached the edge of Sterling. Soon after, Abel entered the city. Surrounded by cramped houses, shops, businesses, he eventually found the right street. He made his way toward the bright electric glow which shone through the surgery windows.

Don't die, small prince.
If you die there will be no bouquets
left in all of London.
—*A.D.*

8

The doctor, named Webb, wouldn't leave till first light. Though Abel was acquainted with Cutland County's regional practice, doctors frequently rotated through, and he was unfamiliar with this one. Older than his predecessors, he walked with a hitch in his step and exhibited less fretfulness. He and his wife gave Abel a room, and lodgings for Tansy in the stables through the back lane. When Mrs. Webb offered him supper, Abel said he had an errand to run.

Going by foot to the downtown, he stopped in at a pawn shop about to close its doors, where he sold his mother's shawl pin. At the grocer's he bought an apple for a dime, which he told the clerk was robbery, and took his time choosing from the barrel.

The cold abating, the snow turned to slush as he walked until he reached a familiar street.

Above the door to Jubilee House was a sign for a soup kitchen. He climbed the stairs, entering a large, crowded room with a makeshift cooking area and a long line of people waiting for food. All the walls had been knocked down. The grandfather clock, opulent furnishings and gilded mirror were gone, the ladies in bright costume replaced by men and stink. In the corner where the pedestal ferns had grown were dark circles on the wood floor. Only the smoke was the same, filling the air in shifting shapes.

Rows of tables were set up like at threshing time. Amidst coughing and low chatter, spoons clinked porcelain and chairs scraped the floor, as men rose from their places to line up for second helpings. Abel realized with queasiness that this might be him a year from now.

He turned to go, but a young man in ratty pinstriped pants with a sallow complexion and wideset eyes blocked his exit. He gestured for Abel to take a seat, and moved down to make space at the table.

Abel sat to avoid offence, while the young man elbowed him and grinned. "Bet you didn't know," he slurped his stew, "this used to be a whorehouse."

Lorelei Schlegel's rosy face passed through Abel's mind. Had she not returned to Germany, had Jubilee House survived, he wondered if by now they would be arguing about Hitler.

Introducing himself as Freddie Teel, the young man asked Abel's name and passed him a bowl of Mackenzie Mash, as he called it — a mix of unrecognizable vegetables in a stock of fatty meat. "It's half rot. Worse than what we got in the work camps."

Freddie went around the table, introducing his companions by their former occupations. "Tubby, there, was in finance. Wallace was an architect. This here is Kurt the chemist and Jo the foreman. Old Lee, if you can believe it, was a professor. The rest of us were nothin'."

The shabbily dressed men nodded at Abel. One was missing a finger, and another a piece of earlobe. Their stench was overwhelming. The more they conversed the more Abel sensed, beneath their toothy half smiles, something boiling over — a restlessness spiked with anger.

Freddie gave Abel a hard slap on his back. "What's landed you here?"

"I'm just pass-passing through." He was careful not to mention his farm. The stew tasted like vomit.

"It's your lucky day," Freddie said. "The almighty prime minister's just announced there'll be work in the big cities for—what's it he calls us?"

"Transients." The architect did not look up from his bowl.

"Right. Mister Mackenzie's offering us street-cleaning duty." Freddie bowed forward in his seat, circling his hand as if to ingratiate himself. "For our highfalutin imperial visitors. Isn't that right, Tubs?"

The man who was once in finance shoved a roll into his mouth, chewed and swallowed.

"Me and the boys are gonna stage a march, if you'd like to join. Another On-to-Ottawa Trek, for George and Lizzie." He spat food in all directions as he spoke. "Imagine their fancy faces. I'll pull those two kings outta that train by their collars myself. We'll swarm 'em till they give us what we want."

Abel cleared his throat. "What— is it you want?"

"Jobs, man. Decent, respectable jobs!"

"I don't think— I read that the R-Railway Act will be stri-strictly enforced. And that the b-bulls will be out with sticks. Come April."

"N-n-never you mind," Freddie said. "That's nuh-nuh-nothing we can't handle. Kurt k-killed a bull. Isn't that right, Kurt?"

"You got no proof." The fellow with matted grey hair glowered at Freddie.

Abel wanted to leave. When someone mocked his stutter it was time to go. Though he partially agreed with the men, their aggression felt extreme. He put his hat on, rose and wished them well.

Freddie followed him out. Abel didn't need to turn around to sense him at his heels. He wished he had brought Tansy, so he could get away more quickly. He wished he had brought his rifle.

"You a monarchist, Abel Dodds?" Freddie squeezed his shoulder. "You giving us airs? You seem to be suffering from... grandiosity."

Hearing a click, he turned in time for Freddie's switchblade to meet his neck. Bringing his face closer to Abel's, Freddie licked his cheek, marking him with his foulness.

"G-go ahead." Abel didn't flinch.

Freddie's pale brows arched. He blinked fast. Lowering the knife to Abel's gut, he took a breath and jabbed. Abel felt only a nick—the blade had barely pierced his skin. Freddie didn't search Abel's pockets, he just averted his gaze, as if he didn't know what to do next.

Gripping Freddie's wrist, Abel pulled out the blade and twisted his assailant's arm. When the knife dropped, Abel pushed him against the wall and grabbed him by the throat, the young man's face going a purplish-red as he squirmed. How light he was, his feet inches off the ground. Maybe a hundred pounds.

Hit by the pungent smell of ammonia, Abel looked down at the urine dripping onto his boot. Looking up again, he realized this was just a boy. A scared, out-of-work boy with no future. A kid playing ruffian.

Abel let go.

Freddie Teel fell to his knees. "Jesus, mister."

Abel picked the blade up off the ground.

"Gimme that back. It was...my dad's."

"Would your d-dad be proud now?"

Getting up, Freddie looked down the street, as if his father stood under the lamppost's feeble light. "Guess not." He rubbed his throat.

Abel felt like a hypocrite. Condemning someone in worse-off circumstances, when his own violent reaction toward Freddie was even more irrational. What was this country coming to? When would it end?

Freddie glanced at Abel's midsection. "I didn't want to do that."

Unbuttoning his coat and lifting his sweater, Abel looked down at the blood on his mother's yellow blouse. "It's not— deep."

His chapped lips pressed into a frown. "No hard feelings?"

Abel reached into his pocket and handed over a dollar with the knife. "I'll have— work in August," he told him. "Come to— Grayley then."

Freddie coughed and spat. "You got a farm?"

"For— now."

"Count me in." He brightened. "If I'm still living." He walked back toward the soup kitchen.

"It was— called Jubilee House." As Freddie turned back to him, Abel nodded to the space above the door where the sign had been.

Freddie gave a wide smile. "I wanted to be an actor. Can you see it?"

It all made sense now. "Sure can."

"How about you?"

"I guess I wanted— to see the world."

"There's always rail riding." Freddie Teel's smile faded. He saluted Abel. Instead of going back into the soup kitchen he called out, "I'll see ya!" and disappeared around the corner.

Returning to the surgery, Abel checked on Tansy and offered her the apple. Sniffing his open hand she accepted it, making smacking sounds as she chewed. Then he went inside through the unlocked back door. The house was dark and quiet. His cut was throbbing, but he didn't wake the doctor. He did not dare delay their departure the next morning. His wound would have to heal on its own.

Alone in the examination room he tried to clean it. Though shallow, it was a messy cut without a precise line, and he had difficulty sewing his skin shut. It took a long time but he managed. Knowing how precious supplies were, he didn't use any dressings or tape. But he did use a little soap to wash the blood from his mother's blouse. Then he slept the sleep of the dead. At dawn he journeyed home to the Wisharts, he and Tansy following behind on the path forged by Doctor Webb and his team of horses.

THIS BRIGHT DUST

Merle came out to put up the animals. Abel made introductions and followed the doctor inside. After hanging his coat and wiping his glasses, the doctor went into the bedroom with his black bag. Una stepped away from the bedside to give him space. Abel stood at the doorway.

"Now then. What do we have here."

"I've given him the usual plasters and tried getting him to cough it out," she said without taking her eyes off her son. "My friend makes a remedy of skunk oil, kerosene and turpentine mixed with lard," she added, "to rub on his chest. But after a few days it stopped working. Then he got a fever."

Doctor Webb nodded. "I'll just take a look, shall I?" He warmed his stethoscope, blowing on it before placing it on Toby's chest. "Fluids?" He listened.

"Spoonfuls," Una told him. "Or he spits it out."

The doctor requested a cup of tepid water. When Una brought it, he extracted a bottle of pills from his bag and dropped one into the cup, stirring with a teaspoon. "This should reduce his fever," he said, "but there's no cure for dust pneumonia."

Sitting Toby up, he propped pillows behind him and tried to get him to drink. The liquid streamed from his mouth. Una supported her son while the doctor tried again, shaking his head. "This county needs a hospital. We should be doing this intravenously."

After the cup was emptied the doctor observed the boy for some time, checking his pulse, listening to his lungs through his chest and back, pulling open his eyelids to assess his pupils with a tiny light. All the while Una sat on the other side of the bed, changing Toby's compresses, rubbing his feet, removing blankets as he sweated.

The gurgling sound the boy made as he took shallow, rapid breaths was unbearable to Abel. He retreated to the kitchen and cursed the sky, and all it unleashed and withheld.

Toby's sickness was brought on by weather. By fine, dry soil particles ripping through the air in the hot months, turning daytime dark as midnight. Winds crackled with electricity. Dust infiltrated homes through cracks, gaps, keyholes, settling on every surface in an accumulation which no amount of sweeping, mopping, wiping could remove. The brown plague, they called his disease. Sucking air from lungs. Abel understood now why he had seen the boy in a gas mask and goggles this past summer, looking like he was heading off to war. The muck must have lingered inside his small body, flaring up now as a winter attack brought on by the cold. He could barely breathe as he lay, possibly dying, in his bed.

Abel was weary of living beneath a sky he could not comprehend. One never knew what to expect when clouds rolled in. Where had this whirlwind he got caught up in with Tansy even come from? It was a summer dust storm and a winter blizzard all in one. The earth was frozen. It had only been snowing. Then dirt rose, as if from a secret place underground. The turbulence of these storms was growing more unpredictable and frightening.

Once Lucie Peloquin had told him, *Your people brought this upon themselves. Digging up grasses whose roots kept the soil together and the plains intact. This wasn't meant to last.*

The sound of a horn disrupted his thoughts. From the Wisharts' kitchen window Abel observed the plow train pushing snow from the track, the sky above fading to a wan nothingness as though it had tired itself out.

Merle came in then. He heated up remnants of stew. Abel took bowls from the cupboard and spoons from the drawer, and set the table, while Merle went and got the doctor and his granddaughter. Doctor Webb rested a hand on Una's shoulder as they all sat down in the kitchen. "We have to give it time now," he told her. She nodded, and the four of them ate in silence.

At the table was a week-old *Sterling Tribune* from February 16, open on a two-page spread devoted to the Royal Tour. Staring at the print, Una broke the silence. "What's going to happen?"

The doctor set down his spoon. "If the dust is too deep, his lungs won't clear."

Merle leaned forward. "Can you take X-rays?"

"We could transport him to the hospital, yes. But that won't change the outcome." He excused himself and stood. "I'll stay till morning, if that's alright. You should all sleep."

Abel cleared the dishes. Una encouraged her grandfather to rest. "Maybe just a few winks," Merle said, and went to the second bedroom.

Una remained at the table, head in her hands. "Brynn was always the driven one. I knew she would go far." She looked up at Abel. "I didn't need to. To be happy."

"Par-pardon?"

"You think I threw away my life. Coming back." She wiped her eyes. "But I wouldn't change that boy's company for anything. This has always been enough for me."

Abel reached for his coat, no longer wishing to intrude.

"Wait." She approached him at the door. "I'm sorry. I'm just tired. Come and sit with us."

He followed her back to the bedroom.

Not once did Una let go of Toby's hand while the doctor continually checked his breathing and repositioned him, trying to lower his fever with more tablets crushed in water.

The boy babbled, the whites of his eyes showing when they flickered open. As the night progressed, his coughing fits lasted longer. Once in a while he spat out greenish phlegm. At the doctor's instructions Abel warmed water and chiseled ice from a barrel outside the front door, going back and forth to the kitchen for clean rags.

At dawn the sun rose crimson, colouring the fields pinkish. By the time Merle woke, Toby's condition had worsened. He became agitated, writhing as he gasped and coughed. The doctor held him down so he wouldn't fling himself from the bed. Then he curled his toes as his arms and legs stiffened under his pyjamas. He emitted a horrifying cry. Abel remembered the badger his father shot one cold night, while he watched. He had aimed for the heart but missed, and the animal had made a piercing sound before burrowing off to die. The next morning, they couldn't track it down. They searched for days, haunted by its death call, and then by a strong odour that led them to the lifeless form. "It'll be okay, son," his father told him. Always that lie. He tried not to think about the badger's stiff body, and open mouth and eyes when they retrieved it from the gully.

Toby stopped moving. His skin was grey. He wasn't coughing anymore. His chest rose and fell in quick succession.

Glaring sunlight came through the window and spread across the wall. When Toby's head fell sideways as they tried to prop him up, Una slid a folded towel between his shoulder and ear. The doctor checked his pulse and turned to Merle. "You should call for the priest."

"We're not calling for anyone." Una looked both men square in the eye. "He just needs rest."

No one contradicted her. She kissed the boy's forehead and hummed. "Winter's almost done," she promised, "we'll soon be picking berries and baking pies. I'll take you to the movies in the city. And I've changed my mind, we can visit Uncle Jake on the ranch. It's not too far."

She cleaned dirt from under his nails and combed his hair. She changed his pyjamas and brought him a beat-up teddy bear. She recited songs from the old family hymnal, while Merle performed tricks of illusion with a wooden wand and handkerchiefs. When Toby started shivering, Doctor Webb draped another blanket over him while Una rubbed his hands.

Abel returned to the kitchen. He thought he should go home and give the Wisharts privacy. Adding fuel to the stove, he searched the cupboards for something to cook for them, but the shelves were bare.

The room began to warm. Merle came out to smoke his pipe. "You mind taking my place?" He picked the paper up off the table. "You could read to him. Anything'll do."

Abel went back into the bedroom, newspaper tucked under his arm, and sat in the empty corner chair. No one noticed him.

"So it— says here," he began, "everyone will need to f-follow royal protocol— when meeting the king and queen. We can't— shake their hands unless they— make the first move."

The boy's eyelids flickered.

"And you'll have to c-call them Your Majesty first, then Sir and Ma'am."

Toby began coughing. Assisted by the doctor, who tapped his back at intervals, he threw up dust and sludge. Una held a cloth by her son's mouth until it seemed nothing was left in him.

"Go on," she urged Abel.

He scanned the article. "Uhh, well— they're making two hundred and fifty— thousand coins." He spoke directly to Toby. "All the schoolkids get one in— commemoration."

Una grabbed the paper and held it up over her son. "Did you hear that, Tobias? Free coins!" She flipped the page. "Look here, you'll like this... a whole section on the princesses!"

Toby's eyes opened and blinked. He looked around the room, pulling his hand from his mother's, giving Abel a small wave before his arm dropped onto the bed.

"Will the princesses be alright in London," Toby asked Abel, "if England goes to war?"

"Of course they'll be alright!" Una rushed to embrace him.

Merle leaned into the room and gave a whistle. "Our boy's got a fighting spirit."

The doctor put his head on Toby's chest to listen, then felt his forehead. He placed his stethoscope below the boy's collarbone, then moved it to different spots and had him inhale and exhale repeatedly. "I proposed to my wife under the king's portrait," he removed the stethoscope from his ears and hung it around his neck, "we're all excited they're coming." He patted his hand. "If you rest now, you'll be in tip top shape for their visit."

They followed Doctor Webb out of the bedroom. "The worst is through," he told them.

Winter, 1939

As he put his coat on in the kitchen, Una pulled a few crumpled bills out from a tin. The doctor pushed her hand back. "I had to pass this way," he said. Just as Abel had suggested he say, the night before, when he paid him.

Una thanked and hugged him then hurried back to the bedroom.

Before taking his leave, Abel made the Wisharts some coffee and left it on the stove.

Then he joined the doctor outside, helped him ready his horses and bid him farewell. Leading Tansy home, he looked back on her every few minutes. Her breaths were laboured but she kept going. He reached into his pocket but had no mints. "The boy— will be fine," he told her. "It was a worthwhile journey." His horse moved slowly, as though each step hurt.

*Someday I'll share with you
a story about a Soldier
of the King and a poet's
bone-white flower.*
—A.D.

9

His body felt heavy—like a big old field boulder—as he dressed and hobbled to the kitchen. Tossing a modest amount of wood into the stove, he made coffee. Through the window, morning unveiled itself in greys. Another day without sun along the east-west line.

As a cargo train passed, Abel looked for Freddie Teel and his band of men. He didn't know why he thought about him. Everywhere were crews like Freddie's—men tired of joblessness and hunger, who'd lost everything and were strengthening in numbers, ready for a revolution. Maybe he should join them. But he preferred doing things alone. In his own time and way.

He put on a second sweater. He could not get warm. He wriggled his toes and fingers, teeth clenched. Nothing was frostbitten. But since returning home from Sterling, his hands and feet had puffed up to twice their size. He'd had to cut off his socks in the night. Now he wrapped the lengths of wool around his toes and ankles, pulling out his cardboard insoles and keeping his boots open. He would tie his laces and put gloves on again, he hoped, within the week. In the meantime, he could do little more than feed the animals and spend the day indoors, enduring pins and needles and the feeling his hands and feet were burning, as his circulation kicked in.

After he milked Elizabeth Moon, freshened hay in the stable and fed the hens, he focused his binoculars on the track. If the coal train didn't come by soon, he and the Wisharts would all freeze. Little matter that February was near over. They would need fuel through spring.

He refocused on the schoolhouse. Its steps were worn smooth from years of children's feet coming and going, his own, Una's and Toby's. To what end? What purpose did a teacherage serve with no teacher? Abel wondered if anyone would miss the backside of the building if he tore it down.

Fetching his tools from the shed, he returned to the house. His father had always wanted a wraparound porch. He even drew up a plan one winter, with thin white planks like piano keys going all around. *What for?* Abel had jested. *You'll have no time to sit once the weather warms.* If only they had built that porch together, it would be useful now.

He was hit with a searing pain in his gut. He picked snow up off the ground, squeezed it into a ball of ice, and lifted his sweaters. Freddie Teel's spontaneous attack was causing him trouble. The snow melted, dripping down his skin.

Inside, he stoked the last embers in the stove and made his porridge, contemplating what his father would have done for heat if things got dire. What part of Grayley would Gilly Dodds demolish?

Abel paced between the two back rooms, wondering how to occupy his time while waiting for his limbs to regain proper sensation. Regardless of whether Toby returned to the schoolhouse once he healed—or whether Abel tore it down for heat—the boy must keep learning.

There were sturdy bedsteads in both bedrooms. He dismantled his parents'—the mattress straw long ago repurposed for livestock

Winter, 1939

bedding — sawing the wood into sections he made smaller with a hatchet. He did the same with the washstand — he could wash in the kitchen sink — adding the intricately carved pieces that were once legs and drawers to the woodpile out front. He also took apart his parents' dresser, transferring its few articles of clothing and jewelry to the Hoosier cabinet.

Licking his thumb, he rubbed the bedroom wall. A damask pattern surfaced under the film of dust. Wiping all four walls down with a damp rag, he peeled a corner of wallpaper back with a knife. It came away easily, glue disintegrating into powder as he pulled.

The least flawed pieces of paper he laid upside down on the floor to sand off leftover glue. Using a plank as his ruler, he cut the sheets into rectangles, making three neat piles. Taking his father's sewing supplies from the smoking table, he sewed each bundle along the spine. Composition books.

Two would go to Toby. One he would keep for his poems.

His pencil scratched across the thick coarse paper. He felt as if he was writing on something important, like an Egyptian papyrus scroll.

Then from his parents' bedroom window he removed the curtains chewed through by grasshoppers, which served no purpose anymore. When he washed the eight small panes of glass in the empty space, they frosted over. Ice formed on the nailheads now visible in the walls.

He closed the bedroom doors. The day was done. He tossed a plank into the stove, his hands blistering and his feet tingling.

At dawn he led Tansy, who pulled a sled loaded with supplies. He left the wood and books, kerosene, milk, butter and bread at the Wisharts' door. He glimpsed Una through the window, head lowered at the sink. Nearby, her grandfather settled into his rocker. As Merle Wishart struck a match and lit his pipe, Abel could practically hear the old man coughing, just as he imagined the sound of Una quietly humming. Merle nodded off. Una went to him, retrieved his pipe and took a puff before setting it on his smoking stand. Going into

Toby's bedroom, she disappeared from view. Abel stood there until she returned to the dishes. Watching her shoulders rise and fall, he felt his throat tighten. Then he made his way home.

Tansy's range of motion was decreasing.

The trek to Sterling had done it. He'd seen this in horses before, joints inflamed with arthritis. This wasn't something an animal recovered from. Light exercise would help her stiffness subside, but she could no longer endure such long rides.

Two weeks passed, then three. February became March. It seemed Una had given up on schoolhouse lessons. While Toby convalesced, Abel didn't see the Wisharts cross the fields. He let them be. What the boy needed for healing was quiet. And warmth. Abel delivered more wood.

One morning after chores, he guided Tansy out for a gentle amble on the snow-covered prairie surrounding the Wise Men.

He had his shovel with him, and here and there he dug, thinking how their livelihood revolved around filling the mouths of these three towering figures. Was it possible his father planted the gold by the grain elevators?

In response to his question, a sound like laughter came from a hole in the earth a few yards away.

Abel approached the hole, wide as a badger's den. A mottled brown face poked out. Laughter again. It was a burrowing owl, whose appearance heralded spring. Abel hadn't seen one in years.

He stepped away and waited. Eventually the bird limped out. A female—he could tell by the plumage, darker than a male's. She cocked her head, looked around and tried to fly. Re-entering her hole, she dragged her broken wing behind her.

She'd be unable to hunt for small mammals like that. If she had a clutch of eggs in that tunnel, her chicks would die. The coyotes would get her.

"Nothing we can do." He gave Tansy a nudge. But his horse, who normally balked at birds of prey, would not move on. For a good half hour they remained like this, Tansy refusing to leave, Abel losing patience.

The little digger stuck her round head out every so often, yellow eyes beaming. Wounded in her trench, she rallied on. Even though, Abel knew, eventually the bird's survival instinct would be snuffed out.

He decided to lie down and doze until Tansy came to her senses. He stretched out on the snow, lowering his hat over his face. The cold soothed his back. He slept a good while, until the owl's peculiar laugh woke him, and a gust of wind blew his hat away. When he opened his eyes, Merle Wishart stood above him, blocking the sun. Merle offered his hand and helped him up.

"Saw you from town," the old man told him, handing him pliers. "Got a toothache. Wondering if you wouldn't mind..."

"How's the boy?" Abel picked up his hat, slipping the pliers into his coat pocket.

"Back to causing mischief. With no memory he bunked with death."

The owl hissed and made a sharp clicking noise.

Merle stooped at the hole. "What've we got here?"

"Her wing's broken," Abel said. "She's as— good as dead."

"That so?" Merle removed the scarf tied around his neck. "Wouldn't want you as my captain. Abandoning your wounded." Reaching in, he pulled the bird out and swaddled it in one move. "C'mon," he told Abel, the owl in the crook of his arm. "Ain't got all day."

Tansy followed Merle and the owl. Abel followed Tansy.

"So tell me. How come I keep seeing you toting a shovel. You divinin' water?"

"I'm— looking for gold."

"Best go to Africa for that."

Abel knew that Merle had fought in the Boer War. But he'd never spoken of it. "Did you— find some there?"

Merle shook his head. "Bravery, dash and courage. All a crock."

Abel brought Tansy to his stable. She extended her neck over the stall door to peer out after he closed it, just as Elizabeth Moon was doing next to her, on the other side of the partition. The cow did not react to the owl. "They're getting old," Merle said.

Abel got a crate from the empty corner stall. Merle passed the owl to him while he lined it with straw. The bird was so light in Abel's hands. He felt like a boy again, trying to nurse a litter runt back to health. Most died, but his father still encouraged him to tend to them, and once in a while one would thrive. There was a lesson there somewhere. Don't believe what you hear. About the small or misshapen ones not coming out stronger.

"We're obliged for the wood." Merle took back the bird. "You get caught pilfering town properties, it's jail time."

"The b-building's falling apart," Abel waved off his concerns. "Needs to come down anyway." A spasm passed through his abdomen and he flinched.

"You hurt?"

"It's nothing."

Merle rested the owl in the crate, which he brought into the house with him. "I'll get her flying." He set her in the corner by the stove. "Plenty of mice around to feed her. Tob'll help." As he knelt to look the bird in the eyes, she lunged at him. He pulled his hand away. "Athena," he said. "We'll call you Athena. Goddess of War." He rose, and sat at the table. "Could do with some of that coffee of yours." He rubbed the side of his cheek. "Before we get down to business."

While the coffee brewed, Abel watched the owl. "How did you m-manage the war?"

Merle stuffed and lit his pipe and took a puff. Smoke climbed the walls, filling the room. Abel poured their coffee and sat across from him, setting the pliers between them on the table.

"I pretended I had powers," Merle said, "for making memories go away. When I left that place, I left the dead there. Said goodbye to 'em all. That's the trick to surviving." He finished his hot drink in one gulp. "See, there's this stupor that comes with battle. No matter which side you fight on. Eventually I felt nothing." He puffed a smoke ring. Reached up and put his hand through it. "Poof. Gone."

Abel knew only what Miss Kitty had taught them about the Boer War—that although the conflict was supposed to be resolved in weeks, it lasted years, with forty or fifty thousand regular folk—mostly Africans and Boer children—dying in British camps.

"Marched across grasslands like ours out there." Merle nodded toward the window. "Every time I look out on the plains, I gotta stop myself from thinking. Fact is, I still dream of the veld. Though mostly I dream of fire." He relit his pipe. "That's one thing you can't blot out with magic. Is dreams."

"Why'd you go?"

"I was young." He snapped his suspenders. "Cavalry paid good. Had no idea what we were getting involved in. Britain told us we'd be fighting to end slavery. Justice against barbarism and all that. Truth was, they wanted the gold republics."

Abel poured more coffee.

"'Course, the Boers weren't innocent, descending from Dutch colonizers. But they were mostly peaceful, just wanting to be left alone. The Empire had us track them, torch their farms, take them from their properties and put them in the camps. Prior to all that, though..." He rubbed his ribcage. "I got hit. Bullet went straight through, so I healed quick. Before going back out, I met some men from D Battery. Had drinks with one of 'em one night. Fella by the name of Johnny McCrae. Ever heard of him?"

"The— poet?"

Merle nodded. "One and the same."

John McCrae was the writer and surgeon who had composed the poem "In Flanders Fields," which Miss Kitty had them memorize. When Abel could not speak the words, she had him write the three stanzas on the board. Even now, he could have written those fifteen lines down in their entirety.... *and in the sky / The larks, still bravely singing, fly / Scarce heard amid the guns below. / We are the Dead. Short days ago / We lived, felt dawn, saw sunset glow, / Loved and were loved, and now we lie...*

"What— did you talk about?"

"All manner of things. He felt conflicted. Believed in fighting for his country but was aghast at how our wounded, and prisoners, were treated. Guess that'd account for why he went from soldiering to doctoring in the next war. Nah, Johnny didn't last long in Africa. I heard he was gone by '01. Before the scorched earth campaign got real bad." He rose and opened the door, as if he needed air. "You go in thinking it's clear who's the enemy. And leave realizing how wrong you were." He rubbed his jaw. "Those Boer troops were little more than boys and farmers and drifters, and we enclosed 'em like cattle. One thing I know"— he turned to Abel— "is Johnny was haunted by flowers long before the Great War. In Africa it was white ones along roads, in fields, in manure. Between bodies. This flower didn't give a goddamn where it bloomed. Johnny called it the cosmos flower. A delicate thing of beauty, attracting bees. There by contam'nation, from seeds come over in feed bags imported for English horses. Johnny was working on a poem. About the pure petals and bright centre, and how the cosmos invaded as the war raged on." His breathing was accompanied by a raspy whistle. "Wonder what happened to that one. The white flower poem no one talks about. Guess his words got lost someplace in Africa." He shut the door on the sunlight and sat back down. "Brought some seed capsules back. That's all I brought with me. Didn't bring back the dead." He spun the pliers on the table. "When we got home, they celebrated us with parades and monuments. Never had public memorials before the Boer War. Then the Great War came and we forgot. 'Cause who wants to recall how we were complicit in all that."

Winter, 1939

Abel got up to rinse the cups.

"Was different for your dad, though, good ol' Gilly." He glanced at the wedding portrait on the radio. "For your dad it was about distinguishing himself and protecting his country. Same as your war. Mine was about our mother country wanting to rule the world. This one's about preventing Hitler from doing the same here."

Abel turned from the sink. "My war?"

"Maybe with your head in the dirt, you haven't heard there's one coming." Merle chuckled.

Abel thought back to when his father talked politics. Gilly Dodds maintained that no matter how critical one felt about their government's involvement in foreign matters, if a far-flung war threatened international stability, one must step up to help secure peace. An isolationist approach was a selfish one. His father also said that the worst thing one could be in such a matter is indecisive. Yet what Abel took from Merle's story, and that of Happy Sanderson, and the poems of John McCrae, was that the main outcome of any war was the suffering of innocents. Why contribute to such abominations? Was it possible to believe in honour and duty without battle? As a farmer, Abel would support the effort by farming, providing sustenance to the allies. Nothing more.

He returned to the table. Merle handed him the pliers, opened his mouth and pointed. Then he gripped the sides of his chair.

When Abel pulled his neighbour's bad tooth the man didn't flinch or cry out or make a sound. His eyes watered a little. Then he took the crate containing his owl and said goodbye.

Abel followed him out. "Did you ever— plant those seeds?"

"Got 'em in a tin. If you want some." He looked down at the owl, nested deep in the straw. "Never spoke of Johnny to no one. S'pose I wanted to keep it for myself. One good moment in the brutality." He levelled his gaze at the big open. "How about that. See the bit of green emerging? How long's it been?"

*I've written you a thousand letters.
Put your hand here. Tear
the envelope of my heart open.*
—A.D.

10

Wet snow came and went again, not lasting, all through March. Abel picked up fistfuls of soil, smelling it and breaking it apart in his hands, feeling for moisture. Searching for the first sign of his winter wheat.

He knew that the secret to the wheat's awakening was patience. He wouldn't make the same mistake others had, not waiting long enough for shoots to emerge, rushing to judgment or panicking and replanting. This year they had not had the ice over the rows that had ruined crops in years past, preventing air from reaching the seeds so they could germinate. He would not reseed too soon.

And now sunup came sooner. Meaning soon the snow would stay gone. Meaning no more choking blizzards or biting cold sleepless nights. Meaning Jake Wishart would soon return home to his family, with money and supplies.

He thought about Toby. That little survivor.

Just last week the boy had come running across the field wearing his gas mask, waving an envelope in the air. With pride he showed Abel the reply to his family's letter, which had arrived by Royal Mail.

He had seen Una standing on the platform with her son on Wednesdays, the day the mail train passed. Waiting, hand in hand, week after week.

For the boy's sake, he did his best to hide his disdain for the king's mass-produced note. His father had received similar formulaic correspondences after the war, conveying King George V's appreciation for his service. Missives Abel later burned for heat. He couldn't encourage Toby's delusions that the king and queen would stop in Grayley, just because they'd received his letter. Thousands of schoolchildren had sent letters. The vague reply — that the king and queen were excited for their journey and looked forward to visiting all Canadians — saved their majesties the obligation of accepting specific invitations. What Toby held in his hands wasn't destiny but chance. One in ten letters would be answered, Abel heard on the radio. That Toby's had landed atop the pile, or been pulled out, was random. It had nothing to do with them personally. A response got printed, stamped and mailed out, with signatures that looked real enough to impress innocent minds. A box got checked in a ledger.

Listening to radio reports of the government's preparations for the king and queen suggested that no international crisis, however great, would change their travel plans. The prime minister busied himself with details of receptions, formal dinners and speeches. Abel concluded that Mackenzie King, who had met Hitler on a trip to Germany two years back and returned to Canada extolling the virtues of their get-together, did not want to think about another European war, preferring to discuss flower arrangements and seating plans with reporters.

Abel railed against the prime minister as he walked his fields in search of growth, hammering sticks in half-frozen spots that would need monitoring.

He was doing this as she neared.

Spring, 1939

He didn't have to look up to know it was her coming. Her steps made a sound that he could not describe, like the sound of pronghorn in sagebrush. Though the animal had not visited in years, his memory of that sound lingered. Especially now, as the earth began its thaw. He supposed it was the sound of hope. At this time of the year, anything seemed possible.

He felt foolish. What did Una want? She had already thanked him for Toby. He didn't want her thanking him again for the supplies he'd left. Neighbours didn't need thanks. They did their duty and got on with it. Anyone else would have done the same.

He stood next to Tansy, her coat so pale now she was almost invisible.

"Our Wincharger broke in the storm." She held out her radio battery. "Can we use yours?"

He dropped the battery into Tansy's saddlebag to take to the small, ragged wind turbine by the barn.

Una stroked Tansy's neck. "Toby is mad for his notebooks. And your coffee is the nicest I've ever tasted."

"It was my father's— recipe."

The wind blew in all directions. "Toby tells me he showed you the letter."

Abel nodded. "He loo-loo— he seems well."

"Oh, yes. He's on the mend." She pulled strands of hair from her eyes. "You know, I could have raised him anywhere. It would have been easier, elsewhere. I came home because I felt more fulfilled here. Even though everyone thought my being a mother out of wedlock was indecent. You too, I'm guessing."

"I never thought—" He swallowed. "I— didn't know—"

"That's just it. People don't always know another person's story. Do they." Her mouth curved into a smile. "At least I didn't have to go to church anymore. Toby saved me from boring sermons. And I'm glad everyone's gone now. All those judgy eyes. They're the failures, not me." She reached for his mare's lead. "They gave up, but we didn't, did we, Tansy girl?"

[111]

As the three of them strolled toward the farmhouse, occasionally Una's shoulders twitched.

"Are you— cold?"

"I don't let my mind stop on it." She blew into her cupped hands. "I still can't believe we got a reply. That this piece of paper, touched, if not by George VI than by one of his associates, crossed the ocean and the country to reach us! A message with the Buckingham Palace watermark and a genuine signature, in an envelope addressed to little old Grayley general post."

Abel had skimmed what Toby had shown him without reading the entire letter. "Did the king— answer your questions?"

"Well, no, it's more of a declaration. But it's a reply nonetheless." She tightened her scarf. "When I think of all the celebrations, parades and ceremonies in the cities, that the radio's going on about... I don't know how we can compete." A line appeared between her brows. "Or maybe they won't visit at all, at the rate Hitler's going. Maybe all this is for nothing."

The sound of an approaching train echoed across the prairie.

The track curved just before Grayley. A slight bend, to accommodate the river. When they were children, watching and waiting for the engine and railcars to come into full view was a thrilling event.

Some trains came from the Yukon and some went on to Oklahoma. Some had a deep whistle and others a shrill cry. At Toby's age, they had come up with names for the trains that served hundreds of farming communities and grain elevators. Dolly was the four-engine locomotive with a yellow caboose. Devil spewed the most ominous smoke. Crazy Lady was the high-speed service with large cylinders. Passengers who travelled in her—women in fox furs— threw pennies and candy at the children running next to the track. Big Bull, which hauled heavy loads, had the largest boiler and a coal man who made funny faces. Toots, the engineer on more than one train, always gave them an extra whistle.

Spring, 1939

In schoolyard games, some trains derailed or were held up by robbers.

Abel wondered if Una remembered any of all that.

As the steam train rolled over the track, he felt its rhythm was akin to a heartbeat. *Boom-boom boom-boom*. Here it comes. There it goes. That's what he always thought.

Una asked to borrow his binoculars. He removed them from around his neck and she handled them with care, leaning slightly against him as she looked out to the rail line.

It was strange to have someone so close. He stood on the thaw, the ground's white curtain opening, while his insides tumbled. Soft light dripped onto them through the mottled sky. A flock of geese passed overhead, flying in a shifting line like a drift of ink. *Boom-boom*.

This was how Abel felt life should be. A glorious March morning. A stint of fair weather, after which one might endure any affliction.

She turned to the schoolhouse. "I wonder where Miss Kitty went," she brought the lenses away from her eyes. "Brynn and I looked for her in Edmonton, asking around in different neighbourhoods. Someone told us she had moved there, but we never found her. She probably married and changed her name. It's hard though, isn't it? When people you love vanish. I still miss my parents daily. I suppose you miss your dad, too, although his illness was no excuse for you to let me win." She handed his binoculars back. "I never wanted to leave here. But you did, and we all knew it." She stared hard at him. "You disappointed me."

Her confession so stunned him that he did not object.

"And don't you dare say it's because he was ailing. We could have helped out and done your fields. It's no excuse. Instead you...you made me go." Her voice became unsteady. "Brynn was the one who always wanted to leave. Not me. I didn't need to go away to keep learning. I can do all that right here"—she pressed a finger against her temple—"and there's no shame in it. Oh!" She looked down. "You're bleeding."

He buttoned his coat. "It's— just a scratch."

They walked without speaking, the remaining snow crunching under their feet. As the clouds dispersed, each patch of soil, mud puddle and pocket of green, every stone and fencepost, and faraway tree, came into sharp relief. You could see for miles. All the way to the vanishing point where the land and sky converged.

"Why are you digging instead of planting?" she eventually asked. "What is it you're trying to unearth?"

"Nothing. I'm only—"

"Trying to get back the past?"

His cut began to throb. He gave his horse a peppermint and offered one to Una.

"It's violent. The way you dig."

They reached the farm. In the stable, Elizabeth Moon greeted Una with a long, drawn-out moo. Una laughed and put a hand on his arm. "It only just occurred to me. You named your cow after Her Majesty!"

Abel scratched his head. "She wasn't— queen yet. When we named her."

"Maybe you knew even then. That Elizabeth would become queen and visit us here. You always were too clever."

He settled Tansy into her stall, and he and Una went back out into the yard.

"I promised Toby a royal banquet." She bit her lower lip. "And a dancing pavilion. When I thought he was going to... well, wouldn't you know, he remembers."

Had she forgotten that their hall and church burnt down? "We have no such— place anymore."

"We could fix one up here. What with your cattle gone." She glanced over at his barn. "Ours is too small. You'll have it back by summer."

Spring, 1939

"That's not — possible." His throat went dry. "The b-barn will soon be taken over by swallows."

"What's a few birds." She reached for his hand. "Do you want to know what I believe, Abel?"

His pulse quickened.

"In a hundred years, no one will recall the depression. Maybe there'll be a page in a book, mentioning farms and the West. But they won't mention us." She let go. "A dance, though, with the king and queen of England, out in the middle of nowhere. I think that's worth remembering." She left in the direction of her farm, calling over her shoulder. "I actually came to thank you. For what you did for Toby. But I know you're not one for thanks." She started walking, then turned back. "You're invited to supper on Saturday. Toby wants you there."

He saw how the path between their houses was becoming worn. A thing the ground recognized and allowed, that the wind couldn't whip away.

With only a few good hours of light left, he decided he should work on the planter's broken axel. He stopped at the barn and went inside, despite himself. Examining the small, cup-like nests attached to the rafters, beams and hayloft ceiling, he tried to imagine what Una envisioned.

Once his father had cautioned Abel about his unrealistic expectations, telling him that no society, or person, could uphold his ideals. That the hopes he set on others were impractical, and impossible for anyone to meet. Or something like that. What Abel had perceived as Una's faults were signs of character and strength. Here was someone who didn't care what anyone thought. Who sought the bright spot, when others dwelled on hardship. Confounding him, like always.

He would need to clear defunct equipment out of the way. Scales and seeders, and obsolete engines. Pumps and churns fallen into disrepair. He'd also have to secure loose beams and patch the leaking roof. Chase off the mice and apply fresh paint. He closed his mind on the whole absurd enterprise, pulling the door shut by its iron ring.

> *Stand with me in the flatland's
> sheen where wounds
> heal to pearly scars.*
> —*A.D.*

11

He wished to start over. As the crocus did each spring. Abel never tired of searching through the disappearing snow for windflowers, as the Peloquins called them. They signalled the end of winter. Purple clusters pushed through the ground in new places every day, retaining the sun's warmth as their petals closed against the nights that were still long.

Rather than seeking out clutches of wildflowers, he should have been trying to assess the growth of what he had seeded in the fall. He had gone against the customary practices of farmers in Cutland County—and the advice of agriculturalists from Ottawa, and western farming wisdom in general—when he had turned all except one of his fields over to fall-seeded crops.

Relying exclusively on winter wheat just wasn't done in the West. "You're a crazy bastard, Dodds," Jake Wishart had said. Winter wheat was for Eastern Canada. Severe temperatures risked too much injury to the seeds and plants here. Experimenting on a few acres would have been fine. Failing on a few acres would not ruin him.

But he had listened to Lucie Peloquin when she recounted how families successfully planted it along the Red River. And he'd heard tales about Mennonite communities harvesting it on the prairies of Manitoba.

He had gone with the Canadian Western Red cultivar, which Lucie advised was the most hardy. Minus the odd Chinook, there had been enough snowpack to insulate what he'd planted.

It was a gamble. Returns were lower. But if he succeeded there would be many advantages. Canadian Red had a higher protein content than its spring counterpart. It was hardier, the yield twenty per cent bigger. The harvest window was wider. He wouldn't have to work under the usual seeding pressures, rushing against time and weather all of April and May. His sowing was already done. He just needed to monitor growth and be vigilant for disease, rust and pests.

The only downfall was having to worry longer—as long as the wheat was in the ground. The main concern, as always, was survivability. Of the crop and of themselves.

And they had survived. The Wisharts, the Peloquins and him. Tansy, Elizabeth Moon and the chickens. The cold would last another month. But the worst of it was over.

Nights were the most bone-chilling. He had moved from his freezing bedroom to the living room for sleeping. But the need for coal and wood was unending. In this way they lived like steam trains, their fireboxes having to be fed constantly to keep moving. At least for now he had a stockpile. Focused on Toby's recovery, the Wisharts hadn't noticed that buildings were missing.

Taking down the first wall had been arduous—the planks seemed to scream out in protest as he yanked and pulled them apart. He had to use all his strength and even then, the wood groaned and resisted before giving way. It got easier with the second wall, then the floor, until he found that this undoing—this exposing the inside to the outside, and tearing wide open—felt good.

Spring, 1939

He knelt at the furry purple flowers. Seeing their bell shapes and yellow centres, and knowing that his friends had returned to their caboose, boosted his spirits. Lucie and Cy were home. In a week or two, the Peloquins would harvest the crocus and use it as a drink to restore energy. As for the leaves, Lucie crushed them to help relieve what she called "general achings."

Abel winced as he checked his bandage. His cut hadn't healed. Tansy's lower legs were causing her discomfort, too. They were warm and swollen, and she was eating less.

He took her bridle from the stable, and got his horse from the paddock. "Let's get ourselves— checked out."

As they neared the Peloquins' railcar, Abel could see smoke rising from the improvised chimney. A few children were outside, raking soil and removing rocks from it, hanging clothes on the line. When he greeted them they banded together with shyness. Lucie opened the door, holding out a fistful of snares. "Rémi, go and set these." A boy ran over, grabbed the wires, and was gone.

Leaving Tansy with the little ones, Abel climbed aboard and hugged his friend.

The Peloquins' red caboose had windows and a cupola. Though there wasn't much room to move around inside, the space was inviting, with high ceilings, a potbelly stove, brocade curtains, a bookshelf and hide mats.

They were still settling in. Crates with dried goods and cookware had yet to be unpacked. It never failed to amaze him how the whole family fit inside, although he knew the eldest ones preferred setting up camp in nearby grasses, coming and going as they pleased. The cold didn't seem to bother the Peloquins as it did others. Or if it did, they did not voice their discontent.

A kettle was heating on the stove. Next to that, the narrow countertop was covered by baskets of white apples, dried berries, moss and a small stack of animal pelts. The family looked more angular than they had a couple of months ago, and Lucie had dark circles under her eyes.

He often wondered how much Lucie missed their farm, though she never complained about how they had been forced to live. Cy complained all the time.

Abel wanted to tell Lucie about Harold Nettles' most recent visit. The roads again passable, the banker had come by to say that foreclosure was inevitable if Abel did not find a guarantor. That he would have to sell the property to pay off the longstanding loans. But he couldn't say anything to Lucie about this. He felt ashamed to be preoccupied with such matters when his friends' land, farm and stock had already been taken.

Lucie pulled out a chair for him and sat back down at the small table, where she was sorting seeds. "You'll be wanting to try a garden again this year." She passed him an envelope to sift through. She dropped seeds into pouches and labelled them. "I heard what you did for the boy. Going and getting the doc in that storm."

Below the railcar's picture window lay the beginnings of the Peloquins' garden. Beyond it, an expanse of dry, cracked earth. "I needed to— go to town anyway."

She poured tea and slid over a plate of bannock. "Eat."

A long time ago, she had told him that her grandparents had survived off bannock when they could no longer hunt, and had to live on government rations on reserves. She didn't fry the bread on the stove as they'd been forced to do, instead using the old way of cooking it over a fire, with dried fruit and without flour.

Abel tore a piece off, chewing slowly. "I came to see— about a balm," he told Lucie. "For me and Tansy."

"Show me."

He pulled up his shirt.

She rose to examine the cut, peeling back the soiled cloth, unfazed by what lay beneath. Turning on the radio, she went to the cupboard, returning with a bottle of clear liquid.

The program was mostly static. He knew the Peloquins charged their battery infrequently—Lucie likely aimed to drown out Abel's potential cries of pain, so her children wouldn't hear. *The*

Spring, 1939

Inter-Departmental Committee's goal for the Royal Tour is for their majesties to meet as many Canadians as they can. It is Prime Minister Mackenzie King's greatest desire to improve relations, while showcasing Canada.

"How do you— feel about all this?"

"It's a good overture. It will confirm..." Lucie glanced up, then back at his wound, "what this country stands for. It's infected."

"Pardon?"

"Your cut. You let it go too long."

Abel tried not to squirm as she flipped her braid over her shoulder, cleaned his skin and scraped pus away with a knife before removing his old stitches.

"Chickens laying yet?" She reached for a needle and thread.

"Should be soon." He grasped the edge of the chair as she sewed him shut. "Now that there's more— daylight."

"Mhmm." She bit the thread to snip it with her teeth. Assessing her work, she poured from the bottle onto a piece of moss, then dabbed his skin with the moss, until the burning sensation turned to cooling.

Cy came in with a trunk and dropped it at Lucie's feet with a grunt. He greeted Abel and studied his cut. "Aie!" He nudged his wife. "How come you don't stitch mine up nice like that, hein?"

While Cy sat and poured himself tea, Lucie opened the trunk, pulling out dresses, coats and even a top hat. "What in the world, Cyril..." she looked up at her husband. "Relief train clothes?"

He sat back, crossed his arms over his belly, and nodded. "All the way from Saskatchewan."

The Peloquin twins, a girl and boy of about Toby's age named Isabelle and Antoine, who had been sitting quietly in the back corner making a finger weaving, rushed over. Antoine pulled out a petticoat. Isabelle reached for a navy pantsuit with gold buttons, and the top hat.

Watching her children, Lucie sorted seeds. Cabbage, carrot, radish. Lettuce, beet, gourd. Her son twirled in the lace undergarment. Her daughter buttoned the coat and petted the beaver fur of the hat. Then Isabelle pulled a pink tulle skirt from the pile, offering it to her mother.

Lucie stared at the top hat.

The children squirmed, looking uncomfortable in their attire. "Take that off," she said in a gentle voice. Antoine kicked off the petticoat and went outside. Isabelle removed the suit and returned to her project in the corner.

Abel had heard on the radio that across the West, Bands were being asked to participate in displays of tribal finery, and to set up improvised camps and teepees for the king and queen to see. There would be dances with performers in regalia. Demonstrations of traditional customs. Chiefs would wear headdresses, and ranchers would recreate old trading posts. A birchbark canoe would be presented to the queen.

Lucie threw the tulle back into the pile of clothing. "I'd rather their majesties see us as we are."

Cy turned to Abel. "How 'bout you, Dodds." He tossed a silk blouse at him. "You like nice shirts."

Abel's breathing came easier. The cut felt better. He eyed a military-style coat in the pile, resembling the CEF greatcoats worn in the muddy trenches of the last war. He could not understand why everyone wore these as fashion now. It was in poor taste. He gave the blouse back to Cy. "I'm fine too."

Lucie wiped the table with one of the frocks, casting it back into the trunk. The radio transmitted nothing but static. Cy shut it off, lit his pipe and opened a week-old paper, offering parts to Abel.

"Where's the news in this? All we got here is stories about king and King. Two kings on one train, osti." He picked tobacco from his tongue. "Meanwhile they got reserve forces using weapons from the Great War."

"I told you," Lucie said, "no more war talk."

Cy ripped off some bannock and gulped his tea. "Inquiète-toi pas, chérie. Me an' Abel here, we got a plan."

His wife bit into a seed. "You two are idiots. If you think disrupting a whistle stop and annoying the prime minister will change anything."

Cy raised his eyebrows, feigning disbelief. "Voyons. Qu'est-ce-que tu racontes?"

She kept her eyes on her husband until Isabelle approached to ask that she tie a bracelet of coloured arrows around her wrist. Lucie kissed her and the girl scurried away.

Leaning over the trunk again, she sorted through fabrics and pulled out a gown of the same pale grey-purple as the crocus. "For Una," she said.

"Abel, why don't you take it to her." Cy smiled at his wife and they laughed.

"I'll do it." Lucie set the gown aside. "He's too bashful."

Abel waited until they had finished having their fun, then rose and put on his hat.

Lucie handed him several packets of seeds. "Let's see to Tansy." She followed him out.

With Tansy's legs balmed and bandaged, Abel and his horse returned home by way of the Horseshoe River, where scales of wolf willow shimmered along the gravel roadside, smelling of spring runoff. The last snowfalls had helped the shrub germinate. Though the riverbed was dry, like Russian thistle clumps of willow still grew in drought conditions. By early summer, once the silver bushes flowered and bore fruit, he'd squeeze out the pea-like seeds and make soup, as Lucie had shown him to do. Crushing a few pungent leaves between his fingers now, he sniffed the musky sweetness before continuing on.

Once home he tried to draw water from the yard pump. He extended his hand under the spout. Nothing. He directed his attention to the barn. Soon it would be occupied by swallows unless he did something. Each year the birds returned to the same nests. Ruined, half-broke nests that they repaired. Even if Abel knocked them down the swallows came back and built new ones. This was their home. They would not forsake it.

Inside the stable, Tansy seemed alright, adjusting to her leg wraps. Elizabeth Moon was also relaxed and grazing, though she was producing only a gallon of milk per day. He then checked on the hens. Still no eggs. Settling in for the night the flock seemed content. "Goodnight," he told them. They continued chattering and murmuring amongst themselves, safe inside their small kingdom.

*Only the old moon knows
that tomorrow's lessening
to a faint, deep-sky curve
won't weaken how I feel.*
—A.D.

12

The air had lost its abrasive edge. Weightless and warm, it carried an intoxicating fragrance, and gave Abel the sensation that he was floating. That evening he walked across the plain to the Wisharts with jars of cream and butter. As darkness came on, the clouds glowed, as though the battery tucked under his arm charged the sky a luminous champagne. Not that he'd ever drunk champagne. But he imagined drinking it now, briefly.

Toby opened the door wearing his mask. The boy took Abel's offerings and set them on the table, then hung his hat and coat. Merle greeted him from his rocker, where he sat smoking, and Una smiled from where she stood at the stove.

In profile, her frame was so thin. He was used to seeing her outdoors, or bundled up in the schoolhouse with extra clothes. At least it was warm in their home, he noted to himself with satisfaction. They were comfortable, then.

The boy approached and stood before Abel.

"How are you f-feeling?"

"Good. You?" Toby's voice came out muffled through his mask.

"I'm not the one— who was sick."

Toby pulled the mask onto his forehead. "Hitler would do away with you." He gave an impish smile. "Because you talk funny."

"Hush, Tobias!" Una said.

Abel laughed. "Probably."

"Did you know he's occupied all of Chilko— Chikusul—"

"Czechoslovakia."

"Uh-huh. Mom says he's going to take Europe next. Then his victory'll lead him here."

Abel pointed at his and Toby's feet. "Right here?"

"Yep. Boppa says Hitler's nothing but a rear area pig. And guess what else."

Abel blew out his cheeks. "What else."

He went to the table and sat, schoolwork spread before him, wallpaper composition book open. "If we were German, I'd be forced to join Hitler's youth."

"No kidding."

Una glanced over but said nothing.

Toby chit-chatted to himself, working out an equation. Abel helped Merle put the battery back inside the radio, then brought the jars on the table over to Una.

Taking a lid off, she dipped a finger into the cream. "Nothing sweeter than Elizabeth Moon." She diced some dried rosehips into fine pieces. "I hope rabbit stew with white apples is alright with you." She sprinkled the fruit into the pot, adding the cream and stirring. Abel wished he could have brought onions, potatoes and carrots. He'd have been a hero then.

Next she mixed cornmeal, Abel's butter and hot water in a bowl, dropping dollops into the frying pan until it cooked crunchy on the outside and soft inside.

Abel was about to offer to whip up his vinegar custard for dessert

Spring, 1939

when they heard a car pull up outside and honk. Una took a step back. Merle reached for his shotgun. "I've had enough of that Harold Nettles harassing us..."

Toby ran to the window, then to the door, jiggling the porcelain knob and pushing the door wide so that it slapped against the house. His gas mask fell to the ground. "It's Lewis!"

With the arrival of spring, Lewis Lyte was back to making rounds in his RCMP Ford sedan. As the Mountie with bulking shoulders and tree trunk legs stepped through the Wisharts' door to wipe his boots on the rag mat, he had to duck so his head wouldn't hit the beam.

"Glad to see you're all alive." Lewis handed Una a bouquet of long-stemmed roses and hung his double-breasted overcoat atop Abel's before placing his hat on Toby's head. "I thought I'd find you all frozen. Had to beg headquarters to let me come. Lucky I didn't get stuck in the mud."

The Lytes hailed from Grayley too. They had all known each other a long time, Lewis having been in school a year ahead of Una and Abel. He was no star pupil. But he always had his hand up with something witty to say, setting the class off in laughter. Before his family moved to the city, he had helped the Wisharts at harvest.

Una held the bouquet like she didn't know what to do with it. Where did such obscene flowers come from at this time of year, Abel wondered? Where else but Sterling.

Lewis went back out to the car and returned with a bag of provisions, unpacking tea, canned beans, chocolate and sugar onto the table. An RAF fighter aircraft for Toby, the farmer's almanac and a bottle of rye for Merle, and periwinkle handkerchiefs for Una. Store-bought scribblers and a box of pencils, which he tossed atop Abel's homemade book.

Well, thought Abel. He had not brought firewood.

Lewis stuck his tongue out at Toby, moving his ears up and down until the boy giggled. Then he handed Una two envelopes. "I checked in on Jake. He and the boys are fine," he told her. "There's talk of a second ranch opening further south. The other one's from Brynn."

She tore the first envelope open and counted a few bills. She read the note, and her face fell. "There's more work than they can keep up with," she said, dropping the letter onto the table. "He'll be home for harvest. But not for seeding."

"We'll see," Merle said.

Una took in a sharp breath. "What do you mean *we'll see*?"

"Jake's got the wanderlust. Ain't so sure he'll come home."

She placed a finger between her eyebrows, closing her eyes a moment. Then she tore open the second letter and smiled, looking up at everyone. "Brynn is graduating! She hopes to work for the sisters by summer."

Lewis winked at Una. "Smart cookie, that sister of yours."

"She certainly is." Una slipped the note into her apron pocket.

While she stirred the stew, Lewis wandered over, hovering too close, in Abel's opinion. When she glanced over her shoulder at the Mountie, her cheeks reddened.

Abel was struck by what a good-looking pair they made. With his fair skin, freckles and golden locks, Lewis Lyte was almost too handsome, like the men in those National Socialist posters. Not only was he charming, he was ambitious and would go far. And where would that leave Una?

Retrieving jars from the cupboard, Lewis poured rye from the bottle he had brought Merle, passing the first to Una with a dimpled grin. Then he brought drinks to Abel and Merle, and they toasted, while Toby buzzed around the room with his new plane.

"What's your official business in the area, kid?" Merle set his jar down on the radio. "They wouldn't send you here just to check on us."

Lewis pushed his chest out. "I've been tasked with investigating a dispute. Between a French and English community further west."

Spring, 1939

"Dispute about what?" Una took the provisions from the table and put them in the cupboard. She also stashed the new scribblers and pencils in a drawer, out of sight.

"Same as always," Lewis grew serious. "The Crown. The war. Conscription."

Abel had no desire to discuss politics with Lewis Lyte. When Toby sat back down, Abel joined him, looking over his work on the table. With a stub of pencil the boy had sketched a train — not a bad rendering, actually — and every now and then he flipped through the encyclopedia, looking up provinces and then jotting numbers above the locomotive's blast pipe.

"Can you add these?" Toby pointed to his column of numbers.

"W-what for?"

"We're calculating how far the king and queen'll go. On their journey." He leaned over the page to fine-tune his drawing.

Abel did the math. "Eight thousand three hundred — and seventy-seven miles."

"Gosh," Toby pushed his chair back onto two legs, making it creak.

Gathering his schoolwork and putting it on a shelf to set the table, Una tipped Toby's chair forward. "You're going to fall."

"Lordy," Lewis rubbed his backside. "It's going to be uncomfortable for their majesties' hind ends. After just an hour, my rear hurts on those seats."

"Don't be silly," Una told him. "The Royal Train will have better seats than those we ride on."

"I sure hope so." Lewis came and sat at the table, resting his chin on his hands as he gazed up at her.

"Do you think they'll stop here, Lewis?" Toby asked.

Lewis brought his hands together into a steeple. "I suppose there's a chance. Although I doubt it. Because of their List of Embarrassing People."

Toby blinked. "Their what?"

"The governor general's office is drafting a classified List of Embarrassing People." He grinned. "Rumour has it your mom is on it."

Merle chuckled. Una set down the pot, reached for her tea towel and swiped Lewis on the shoulder.

He was right, though. About the top-secret list of shameful individuals. Abel had heard as much the other night, in a report outlining security protocols for their majesties. To ensure the king and queen's safety, guards would also be on the lookout at every railroad crossing, bridge and tunnel as their train passed.

As an extra precaution, a nondescript pilot train filled with RCMP and reporters would run a half hour ahead of the Royal Train. Were there any bombings or attacks, those on the pilot train would perish, while the royal party remained at a safe distance.

"Will you — be on the p-pilot train?"

"Nope. I put in a request to patrol these parts." He saluted Toby. "I also had the honour of accompanying two blokes from Scotland Yard's Special Branch in February, who came out to inspect the tracks. 'Bloody hell, it's cold here,' they kept saying. 'Bloody hell!'"

Toby's eyes widened. "Wow."

Lewis got up and went over to the stove, lingering again next to Una. He could not sit still. After sampling the stew he retrieved the new carton of salt from the cupboard and dropped some in.

Una wiped up what he had spilled on the counter. "Would you like to stay for supper?"

He nodded. "That'd be swell."

Ushering him back to the table, she set another place and began serving.

"Of course, the Yard's not too keen on the timing of their majesties' visit, due to the Nazi threat," Lewis tousled Toby's hair. "Plus the king's got health problems. But the closer Europe comes to war, the more Chamberlain's fixed on their coming."

"And what's the consensus," Merle asked between spoonfuls, "around these parts?"

Spring, 1939

"There's reports of hostile attitudes. But not to worry," Lewis pointed at Abel, smirking. "I'm keeping an eye on suspects." He reached for a second puck of cornbread. "Overall, there's excitement. And the souvenirs are bonkers. Police can't keep track of all the merchandise being produced, so it's been decided to let people sell what they want. Government even lifted the ban that forbids the reproduction of their majesties' likenesses." He nudged Toby. "Except, their portraits aren't allowed on candy wrappers. We don't want the king and queen's faces drifting around with garbage."

"Obviously." The boy watched the Mountie's every move.

Una didn't say a word. She ate her stew and glanced at her brother's letter, which remained on the table's edge.

The tablecloth held deep creases, as though it had not been used in a long while, the ivory cloth scattered with holes, through which the table beneath was visible. The oil lamp flickered as it grew dark outside, and the room's shadows grew.

The Wisharts ate mostly without speaking. Abel savoured each spoonful, tuning out Lewis's slurping, which reminded him of Freddie Teel at the soup kitchen. As the Mountie sucked and slurped, Toby giggled and covered his mouth with his small hand. Una pressed her lips together as she looked down at her bowl.

After he finished, Lewis wiped his chin on his brown tunic sleeve, reached across the table and squeezed Una's arm. "How about a little dancing?"

Toby leapt up. "Yahoo!"

"Oh, no. Not for me." She began collecting plates. "I haven't danced in years."

Merle poured another round of drinks and switched on the radio, turning the dial until he found some swing music. Abel's palms grew sweaty. He had only ever danced with his father in the kitchen those winters their house became an icebox, as a way to keep warm. He rubbed his thumbs. He had filed his fingernails before coming. Brushed them with a coating of egg white, and buffed them till they shone clean.

Lewis rose from the table, took the plates from Una and set them back down. Grabbing her hand, he led her to the middle of the living room, where they swung each other around. Una studied his feet and followed his lead until she had her own rhythm going, both of them moving apart then together, then apart, as they flew around the room.

"That's the Lindy Hop," Lewis said after the song finished. When Toby rushed over to dance with his mother, she tried to sit back down, but Lewis pulled her up from the table again, despite her protests.

"Make us some coffee, Abel?" She called over her shoulder. At the end of the next song, she escaped to the table. Catching her breath, she fell back into her chair.

Merle tapped a foot while Lewis and Toby danced. Soon Una was laughing. She held her hands up to her cheeks. "Thank you," she told Lewis, "for showing me how sorely out of shape I've become."

"At your service." Lewis bowed and straightened, then reached for her hand and kissed it.

She stood and switched off the radio. "Well. I think that's enough for one evening."

Abel poured coffee as she cleared the table.

"So." Lewis's forehead gleamed. "The Peloquins still dwelling by the rails?"

Una whipped around from the sink. "They're doing nothing illegal."

"She's right," Merle said. "Leave 'em be."

Lewis flashed a smile. "I only wondered if I needed to verify their well-being."

"They d-d-don't need anyone checking in."

Lewis made a face as he drank his coffee. "Oof. Hope you don't mind if I don't finish." He set the cup down and went to the window. "Probably too late for me to drive back now," he turned to the Wisharts, frowning, "with no moon to light the way."

Toby ran to Una and tugged her arm. "Can he stay, please?"

Spring, 1939

Merle sank into the sofa, which was covered with a quilt of muted colours. "I'm good here."

"I suppose you can take Jake's cot." She sighed. "If you don't mind sharing."

Lewis's eyes narrowed at Toby. "You don't snore, do you?"

Before heading home, Abel looked in each of the front room's four corners. "Where is your owl?" he asked Merle.

Merle glanced at the boy, who spun around from Lewis to hear his great-grandfather's answer. "Athena? Oh, she flew off. Almost straight away."

Lewis slapped Abel on the shoulder. "So long, Doleful Dodds. Careful out there."

Abel got his coat from under the Mountie's and picked up his hat, which had fallen on the floor. "Thanks— for dinner." The Wisharts barely glanced up, everyone immersed in the deck of cards Lewis was dealing.

Leaving them to their game he went out into the night. He hadn't thought to bring a lantern. But when he looked up he could see by the stars and cut of moon just fine.

> *One day we'll forgo the part*
> *of ourselves we can't recover*
> *and travel to a new grassy realm.*
> —A.D.

13

The days lengthened, and gophers poked their heads from burrows. The more the light stretched out, the more intense was Abel's hunger. At dawn and dusk when wildlife roamed, he walked the fields in search of deer, pheasants, turkeys—once considered a nuisance for feeding on crops. The animals who had fled the battered countryside at the start of the decade had not returned. No one would have newborn stock this spring either. No calves, colts, lambs or chicks. Only rabbits, rodents and blackbirds.

He saw no migrating flocks. The burden of the thought of shooting birds from the sky lifted. Stomach grumbling, he deliberated killing one of the hens—roasting it crisp with butter and breadcrumbs—then shook off the idea. Besides, the chicken meat would probably taste like grasshoppers.

Though the grasshoppers were gone, he tasted them in everything. At first he had fried them for protein, but they carried a stink like turning meat. Chewing and swallowing salted pieces, he felt them crawling around his insides as if they were still alive to the end.

The grasshoppers arrived in the early part of the drought, the year Abel's father died, and they stayed three years, consuming ripe wheat leaves, stems, grains, hay. Abel blamed them, in part, for his father's death. Gilly's anguish about the infestations weakened his immune system. A forbidden newspaper circulated among patients, where he read about the damage the insects were inflicting on the countryside. He asked Abel about them and had him sneak some into the sanatorium in a jar, with a small sack of wheat kernels, so that he could study their voracious eating behaviour.

The grasshoppers made Abel feel he was going mad. He banded together with other farmers to combat the swarms with nets, traps and expensive and poisonous pesticides. They burned stacks of good straw to smoke them out, but the grasshoppers prevailed, chewing through fields, clothes on the line, paint on buildings. Chewing through his hair. Chewing the sun to blackness.

It had been a few years since the last outbreak, but on occasion Abel still had the distinctive sensation that he was stepping on them, squishing their bodies fat with wheat. He imagined their slime and the stink. He could still hear them chewing, landing on the rooftop and smacking against the windows with the impact of hail, millions of deafening thuds. Creeping in his bedsheets, clouding his dreams, jumping into his mouth, eyes and ears.

Since the grasshoppers, Abel always began his early spring weeding with a sense of unease. Sometimes he would find a harmless exoskeleton and would crush it swiftly. Even after combing the soil for egg sites, finding none, he remained anxious.

There wasn't much to weed yet. It was still too early in the season.

Through April, as the air warmed and the soil softened, he dug holes in search of his father's bullion. He collected wood and coal. He worked on an old broken truck, walked the fields and shovelled sand from the fence line.

Spring, 1939

When he ran out of things to do, he pulled seed from a dark corner of the barn, dusting off sacks of crested wheatgrass the government had distributed the year prior, for grazing land and hay. He would test it out in the one field he had left fallow.

It was called Fairway Wheat, and was supposed to thrive even in the cold and without moisture. Even with frost. As the story went, the scientist who developed it found the seeds by accident in an office drawer and cross-pollinated them with another type of seed to create this new strain of grass. The seeds came from Siberia, which shared the same harsh climate as the prairies.

Abel filled his old two-cylinder with gas he had acquired for a pittance from Cyril. How he fantasized about having a six-cylinder Model B with a diesel engine, rubber tires, an electric start and lights! But his clamorous machine still got things done.

Pouring the seeds into the grain box, he attached the cultivator-seeder to the tractor. The seeder worked by breaking up the soil, making seedbeds, dropping the seeds and protecting them with a soil layer. He started the engine and progressed across the field in a linear path, each pass intersecting with the previous one to leave no gaps. Cultivating and planting at once, it took under a day to sow the whole area. Working the land again after the gruelling winter, Abel felt a renewed sense of purpose.

In the late afternoon, just as he finished, he saw a lone figure seated on the bench at the station. He walked along the track, passing through Grayley. On the street broken open with cracks and overrun with weeds, false fronts of empty stores tilted forward like grave markers on shifting ground. He could still read signs behind the accumulated grime of those windows that had not been boarded. *Today's Special: Rhubarb Pie! Firewood & Lumber Sale This Week. We Mend Clothes, Reliable and Affordable. Saturday Hall Dance! Live Band, Get Tickets Here.*

At the end of Main Street he reached the station platform, climbed the steps and approached Una. She was wearing Jake's work clothes and hardly looked up when he sat.

"They're calling it the palace on wheels," she said. "Isn't that pretty? They'll have air conditioning, oak-panelled rooms and a switchboard to call the princesses at Buckingham Palace. Oh, and a barbershop! And even a little library."

Abel had heard about the dream train's lavish living quarters. "They say that library will con-con— will have a translation of— *Mein Kampf*."

"Yes, well. I suppose they need to study his lunatic mind. Even from here."

She had missed the latest news, then. Abel thought the Wisharts probably limited their radio listening to evenings, to save battery power. In which case she would not have heard the CBC's announcement, that very morning, that the tour was as good as cancelled. Hitler was strengthening ties with Japan and Italy, and Britain and France were mobilizing troops.

On hearing the conjecture about the tour, Abel had felt relief. Now, though, he felt a nagging doubt that the change of plans was for the better. For Una, anyway. And Toby.

He held his hat in his hands. "It seems the tour likely won't— transpire."

"Chamberlain says international affairs are stable." She looked into the middle distance. "The king and queen set sail in a few weeks."

He was unable to read her emotional state. Her lack of reaction indicated that perhaps she too, had heard the news. "That— was yesterday. Today he's p-preparing for war."

"I have faith. Their majesties aren't quitters." She stayed quiet a while. "You know, I almost quit once. It took me by surprise. I never saw it coming." She turned to him. "Have you ever done something over which you felt you had no control? It felt like I was watching myself from above." She laughed, shaking her head. "And

Spring, 1939

I was astonished by what I was doing!" She pulled a handkerchief from her pocket—one of the dainty ones Lewis had given her. "Remember that summer? The hottest, driest one, 1936, when the air was like a furnace and our candles, radio knobs and shoe soles melted? Along with the seals on jars, our toothbrushes and my one pair of nylon stockings. It was so hot that day I felt delirious, standing there washing dishes with a thimble of water as the morning train approached. Grandad and Jake were out in the fields, Toby on Jake's shoulders. Without knowing what I was doing, I put down the plate and dishcloth, took off my apron, pinned my hat, rushed for my purse and ran all the way here, boarding without even a ticket. When the conductor came through the carriage, I hid in the lavatory. Have you got a cigarette?"

Abel shook his head.

"Never mind." She slowly exhaled. "Once I got to Sterling and made my way to the street corner, it felt as though all the traffic and pedestrians were looking me over as they passed. Had I become that shabby? Women my age went by arm in arm, carrying shopping bags and whispering. They didn't seem poorly off compared to us. The heat didn't seem to bother those city girls, either. I must have wandered at least an hour on those blazing sidewalks, until I reached a hotel. It was next to a bawdy house, but I didn't care." She gave him a sideways glance. "I took a room there, paying with egg money. It was stuffy, with moths under the lampshade and artificial flowers on the nightstand. Then I dialed room service and ran a cool bath. When my food arrived, I slipped into the tub to eat my hamburger and drink my bottle of beer. Through the wall I heard voices of men and women entertaining each other. I could guess what kind of establishment it was. The kind Jake frequents."

"I'm sure he— doesn't—"

"Don't patronize me, Abel." She stomped a foot. "You really take me for an imbecile, don't you. Anyway, after the bath I lay on the bed, staring out the window while the fan above cooled my skin. Flies buzzed around, cars honked and people went by as if through a turnstile, their heels *click click clicking* like mine did on this very platform when I left my life behind." She stared down at her boots. "I thought then that I might stay in Sterling forever." She looked up again, blinking. "It was during the grasshoppers. Those damned insects made me crazy. When Toby coughed, I thought it was grasshoppers stuck in his lungs. By then I believed the grasshoppers would never leave. Not till they consumed our last breath."

Abel wanted to jump up and say, *I felt the same!*

"I blamed everyone around me. I blamed grandad for being too easy on Jake. And I blamed Jake for devoting his attention to cattle while neglecting the crops. I blamed my parents for getting sick and dying. And I blamed Brynn for... well, that is to say, I used to blame my sister for a lot of things. Then I heard a boy's voice in the hallway, and that made me think of Toby." She looked down the line then back at him. "Who was a gift to me. Do you understand what I'm saying?"

He swallowed. "Yes."

She waited, as if expecting more. But what more could he say? She wanted him to know how much she loved her boy. He understood this as something requiring no explanation.

"Alright then... good." She fiddled with her handkerchief. "Well, here I was abandoning him. I tossed and turned but couldn't sleep. Lying there, I realized it was no use. I had to let the past go and do my best. Staying angry only led to poor decisions. And sleeplessness. So I got dressed and left the hotel, and visited an art gallery." She crossed her arms, hands on elbows. "Inside, I walked through rooms of nature landscapes, winter scenes and fields of flowers, stopping at a small painting showing a great rock in the sea with a hole in it. And it was as if that stone had a soul. The hole made me think of what was gone... especially my old self. It made me think of a needle threaded by water. I saw how stone could endure anything. Fire. Battles. Bombings. Plagues of grasshoppers. I stood before that small canvas an awfully long time, until my life no longer felt ruined."

Spring, 1939

Abel thought of the stone feather he had unearthed, both hard and delicate, now on his sill. She tucked her hair behind her ears. "After that, I stopped at a diner, ate a piece of cherry pie and took the train home. I only had a dollar left." She rose to go. "I still sometimes wonder if staying is pure folly. But I made my decision that day. I don't think there's any better place. I'm grateful for what we have here."

They walked homeward together, and she stopped, considering the schoolhouse up ahead. "Remember when Miss Kitty unlatched the Dutch door every spring, so that the top half stayed open to let the classroom breathe? I always looked forward to that." The windburn rose on her cheeks. "I don't suppose we'll go back now. There'll be too much to do with planting. But that's fine. It's all going to be fine." She spoke as though trying to convince herself. "The thing is. There's so much to worry about these days, I don't know what to worry about first." She looked to the horizon. "Why bother with any of it, is what Jake thinks. Why bother sowing our own failure, when the price of wheat is still below the cost of seed. He always wanted to leave this hardpan county. Just like Brynn. Well, they can stay gone. Neither of them ever wanted the farm anyway." Reaching down, she picked up a fistful of dry grass. "Harold Nettles agreed to push our loan deadline. And the Feed and Seed's extended our credit. Jake doesn't need to be here. Grandad's already suggested I take charge."

She stood there, as exposed to the wind as the fields, all the protective layers blown off. Jake was leaving things up to her. Every decision and consequence were hers alone now. Abel knew well how this felt. He calculated in his mind. She would have to get the seeding done in the next few weeks to harvest by August—a near impossible task to accomplish on her own, even if the weather cooperated.

She pulled a booklet from her coat pocket. *Soil Drifting Control in the Prairie Provinces*. Abel had the same one from the Dominion Experimental Farms. Everyone had received these in '35.

"I'll strip it," she said. "Jake wouldn't hear of leaving land fallow. He wanted nothing to do with new methods. Even when prices plunged, he refused to plant rye and flax. Well, to hell with him for not listening to me."

Abel had tried stripping, without much success. But he also saw how set Una was on proving her brother wrong. "Strip farming will t-take half the time," he said. "You may actually— get a yield. And reduce drift."

"All I've got to do is make edges." She flipped through the brochure. "Winds mostly blow west to east, so I'll run the strips north to south, making them eighty, maybe a hundred feet wide..." Her thoughts trailed off as she studied the fine print.

"I c-c— I'm happy to help."

"I'll manage. You've got enough to do."

The Wisharts' John Deere had been repossessed and lay in a storage depot with hundreds of others. "At least," said Abel, "take my tractor."

She waved the thought away. "I know how to work our two horses. Dukey could use the exercise. We'll plow and seed with grandad's help."

"You'll never— get done in time."

"Tomorrow I'll grease the axels. And start on some practice runs." The setting sun crested over the treeless plain, bathing them both in soft light. "Do you know what I constantly ask myself these days?"

Abel waited.

"It always helps me through. I ask myself, *What would the queen do?* The queen would buck up and carry on. If there's one thing I'm sure of, it's that."

Acres of shadow stretch around us,
changing shape by the hour.
After the storm, torn wings.
—A.D.

14

From afar, the Wisharts' daily activities unfolded across the flat land like pages of a story. Merle and his great-grandson went in and out of the barn, house and implements shed, while Una worked the dry soil, contending with stubborn horses no longer used to heavy labour.

First she had to pull the disc and plow through the earth. She did the same thing with the planter. Her team of two horses did not want to skip sections. They balked and tried to go in reverse when she urged them to bypass the next line. On they went, with Una struggling behind them, going forward then backward, making a mess at the end of each row. But not once did she quit, or send Toby over to ask for Abel to join in.

He knew how her neck and shoulders must have ached by the end of that first week. By the end of the second, he could feel her hand blisters bleed through her gloves. Even with goggles, the dust would blacken her skin, burning her eyes, lodging itself on her scalp and under her nails. But she kept going, and her team got used to skipping rows.

Though the sun nourished them with honeyed warmth, the late April nights were still cold. Abel still wore a coat on his evening walks under the star-filled sky. It made him think about the colander he'd placed a candle inside and hung from a nail on the wall as a boy, trying to replicate the glittering prairie darkness. The Wisharts said they lacked nothing. But even once the nights warmed, they would need fuel for cooking. Abel would make sure they had it until Jake came home.

Keeping a close eye on his plants, and dealing with the suddenly relentless weeds, he took down two more walls to top up his neighbours' woodpile.

During the teardown, he found a dragonfly settled between two slats. With his pinkie he dislodged the long body. It had probably been on its way to the river. The dragonfly changed colour as he held it up to study the slender legs, large eyes and transparent wings. Going from blue to green to brown to yellow in the demolished room, until the wind blew the insect from his palm.

He did away with another chunk of floor. Pilfering, as Merle called it. To Abel it felt more like returning the land to its natural state. Making space for more growth, while Merle and Toby did the opposite, building up and brightening Grayley's storefronts with whitewash. Reviving the station's exterior.

In her family's movements Abel could see Una's desire to make do. To create an illusion of a flourishing place. To pretend for the king and queen of England that hard times were done.

The third week—by this point it was early May—he observed Una through his binoculars. She had tied the reins around her waist, and she walked behind the horses and plow. It was an old trick. As she grew tired, the horses would pull her along. It was a dangerous manoeuvre. Thinking of all the bones she might break—or worse—kept Abel awake all night. In the morning, he went over to insist she accept his help.

Spring, 1939

Knocking and getting no answer, he let himself into the farmhouse and found Toby on the ground, playing jacks. Una sat in her grandfather's rocker, holding a compress over her eyes. She peered out from under the cloth. "I tried making your coffee."

"But it tastes awful." Toby bounced his ball, plucked a jack from the pile and caught the ball before it landed.

Abel cleared his throat. He had prepared what to say. *You can't go on without assistance. That's what I'm here for. At your service. I have a plan for dividing up labours.*

She rose to start the day's work. "You've done your part. Keeping us stocked. I don't know which farms you're stripping, but you're bound to get arrested." She put on her coat. "And where will we be, without you?"

"I h-h— I want to propose—"

She turned, her face open and vulnerable. Like she would listen to anything he had to say. She had never looked at him in that way.

Then Merle came in. "There's one coming," he said. "There'll be no planting today."

They went outside. Along the horizon a moving ridge of grit took over the sky. The air got heavy. As the swell rolled toward them, Abel smelled that distinct, musty odour of a dust storm in the brownish-grey mass.

He should have known. In the last day the temperature had warmed by fifteen degrees. They'd had dust storms before in March. Why not now in May?

Toby dashed into the yard for a better look at the menacing, dense cloud, until Una pulled him back inside. She grabbed his mask, and fastened it down over his face. She pointed to the table. "Don't move from here."

Abel and Merle ran to the barn to put up the two horses, give them extra feed and close the shutters. Returning to the house they boarded the windows and lay damp rags in every crevice, covering their faces with handkerchiefs.

Then Abel stepped outside again and took one last look at the smothering cloud coming in. Within its depths coursed a buttermilk light. It was illogical, how something so destructive could be so beautiful. Part of him wanted to stay in the middle of the yard and await the storm's fury. He was mesmerized.

Having no time to get to his own property, he returned inside to wait with the Wisharts in their darkened house.

On the radio, William Aberhart delivered a razzle-dazzle sermon, playing the mandolin and condemning fascists. Merle shut it off. An hour passed, then two. They sat by the stove, listening. What they listened for was a buzz, a rumble, a bursting. They listened and listened, and still no storm came.

By dim kerosene lamp they stoked the heater, played cards and ate pouding chômeur, waiting for the roar. Eventually Merle fell asleep in his rocker. Toby read from the almanac. Abel made coffee and sat at the table with the boy and his mother. Una worked on numbers until finally, rubbing her temples, she shut the account book. "I can't take this," she said, and rose to open the door. Merle woke, and they all followed her outside.

There was nothing to see but a greenish pall of white sky, with no debris. The sound of meadowlarks.

"I don't understand," she said.

Her grandfather rested his hand on her shoulder. "I s'pose they're finally losing strength."

Abel returned home. It was already midafternoon. He checked on Tansy and Elizabeth Moon, who were quieter than usual, and the hens, who would not leave their coop though he urged them to come out into the day.

The murky green tint over the sky wasn't going away. It gave him a funny feeling. He boarded the windows with plywood, covered the truck he'd been working on with sheets weighed down by rocks, and secured the animals before going in to make porridge for supper.

It came at night, hours into the gloom of sleeplessness.

Spring, 1939

From his mattress on the living room floor, where he lay listening to his beating heart, a louder sound emerged—the long-drawn-out howl of the wind hurtling by, whipping dust through the roof, sides and floor of the house with such force it created an intense pressure inside Abel's ears. Even as he covered them, he could not block out the roaring. A barrage of debris struck his house, front windows cracking behind the plywood, shingles overhead flapping and ripping off the roof. The porcelain pigs rattled on the sill. His parents' wedding portrait fell from the radio. Soft thuds sounded from outside like bodies of birds being thrown against the wood siding. The worst sound of all, beneath the din, was the gentle undercurrent of a repetitive *tap-tap-tap-tap-tap-tap* as a stream of seeds hit the side of the house before blowing off into the atmosphere.

He felt the storm's sandpaper texture on his bare feet when he rose and lit a candle. Even if he couldn't look outside, he knew the wind was making dunes and obscuring the stars. He waited at the kitchen table with a wet rag covering his mouth. The doorknob rattled. Another gust blasted through, which shook and seemed to lift the house from its foundation, and Abel held fast to the table's edge and thought *one day one day one day I will tell my children about this*. The pillowcase curtains billowed up against the ceiling, one of the pigs tipped over into the sink, and the other seemed to fly—landing on the floor, breaking. A final exhale from the wind snuffed out the candle's flame.

Abel stepped into the ashen dawn, grounding himself by touching the nearby trough to discharge static electricity.

The whole year's work was undone. The storm had uprooted his newly sprouted winter wheat. The Fairway seed he'd planted had blown away with the topsoil. The schoolhouse was blackened, along with the whitewashed Main Street. The middle grain elevator—the greatest, most impressive tower—had fallen.

He walked through the furrows of flattened and broken shoots. The storm had likely decimated all his crops. He scooped up soil interspersed with pale and golden-brown grains. Seeds from the Wishart farm had drifted over, mixing with his. A thick fog of dust dampened the sound of his movements. It would take days to settle.

At least the stable and barn still stood. At least Tansy, Elizabeth Moon and the chickens still had a roof over their heads. Although they were jittery, he brushed dust from their coats, mouths and eyelashes. Removed silt from their buckets, gave them water from a covered drum to drink and bit the insides of his cheeks to keep himself from falling to his knees.

At this late stage it would be next to impossible to start over.

Merle arrived then. "Just came to see you...made it through." He sat on a bale. Abel sat next to him.

"It's like war," his neighbour said. "You wait. And the waiting gets monotonous. The anticipation's so tiresome you grow bored. Then *bam*. Devastation. The world turned upside down." He pulled a stem of hay from the bale and slipped it between his teeth. "Nothin' we could've done."

Abel walked back with him through their ravaged fields. Inside the Wishart home, Toby crouched under the table in his gas mask, drawing stick figures in the sand with his finger while Una swept piles of sand into corners. When she saw Abel, she sat. "We're finished," she said, her voice barely audible. "We'll have to go to the city. And move into a charity house. Everything's gone."

Merle poured a couple fingers' worth of rye from his bottle into three jars, and passed them around. He switched on the radio. After such apocalyptic storms, Abel believed that the prairies should still headline the news, like they had in the early thirties. But no one was interested in dusters anymore. Millions of tons of soil being carried across the plains no longer generated attention. This environmental disaster, which had laid waste to what remained of Grayley, would never be thought of or mentioned. Anyone who cared was right there in the room.

Merle raised the volume.

Spring, 1939

Again, we have confirmation that their majesties will set sail on the sixth of May. The king's request to make a personal appeal to Hitler has gone unanswered by the British government. Amid growing uncertainty over Chamberlain's appeasement tactics, perhaps King George believes that a diplomatic mission to Canada will be more beneficial than waiting in his palace? We'll discuss all this in the next hour.

Coming out from under the table, Toby raised his mask up onto his forehead. "The tour's not cancelled?"

Una pulled the mask back down over his face, sat him in her lap and shushed him while they listened. King George and Queen Elizabeth would leave their battleship behind, in case the navy needed it—there had been sightings of the Germans off the Spanish coast. They would make their crossing in the *Empress of Australia* instead.

"What if there's enemy subs in the water?" Toby hopped from his mother's lap.

"It's— reckless to come," Abel said. "They'll— get torpedoed."

Una stood, and drifted around the room with a faint smile. Rubbing dust from her eyes, she kissed her son's head. "This trip is important to them," she said. "They're courageous." She opened the front door. "We have to clean up. And try again." Returning to the kitchen, she soaked rags in water to tie around their faces.

Abel leaned against the doorframe. Leaves hadn't had a chance to form on his winter wheat. His Fairway grass hadn't grown. The damage was irreparable. His fields no longer mattered. He turned to the Wisharts. "Let me help."

Toby looked up at his mother. Surveying his granddaughter, Merle took another drink. Una did the same, then said, "Alright."

A bird swooped in through the open door.

"Swallow!" The boy chased the bird until it disappeared out into the dim again. He turned to his mother. "That's good luck!"

Many times, Abel's father had told him if a bird found its way into a house, it meant someone would die. That birds travelled with spirits from one world to the next.

He stepped outside in time to see the murmuration passing overhead. He had no word for the birds' iridescent blue. Watching them, he wondered how they flew in such close proximity, moving through the dirty sky like a ribbon.

> *Sifting through wreckage*
> *for treasure, your faith*
> *a ship sailing the cloud line.*
> —A.D.

15

The middle grain elevator was gone, and a trick of the eye made the remaining towers look closer to one another. They came into Abel's view like two people standing side by side, not touching. The storm had made the landscape's distant objects seem indistinct, as though set in a mist. Across the way, the Wishart property appeared fuzzy. As particles of dust settled and the sun emerged, a reddish tint spread over the ground.

Each day after tending to Tansy, Elizabeth Moon and the hens, Abel walked over to his neighbours' and dug sand from their fields. Cy Peloquin also came to assist when he could, while Una sent Toby off to learn with Lucie's children. As usual, the Peloquins had gotten by, having covered their small plot with tarps before the wind came. Owning next to nothing offered advantages, Cy joked.

In the aftermath of dust the wind persisted, though less forcefully. The sea of sand was interminable. Scooped away, it blew back again hours later. Shovelling and raking, day after day, they choked on sand and spat it out.

Eventually the wind let up. They made pits, blocking the sand with rocks so it couldn't fly back in their faces. The dust tossed in stayed in, and that was something. Afterwards they tried tilling to replant, digging and stirring and overturning, which created more dust. Una brought out a sleek new portable radio, a gift from Lewis, so they could listen while working. The next two weeks passed in this way, with Abel crouching in the fields alongside the Wisharts, seeding in the sandy dirt, praying for rain. But the sky stayed as cobalt-blue as the darting swallows overhead, which increased in numbers as the days progressed, performing their aerial ballet.

Reports of war preparation lessened as accounts of the royal arrival took over the airwaves. Especially after the sixth of May, when King George and Queen Elizabeth left Buckingham Palace with their girls. At Waterloo Station, they told their daughters goodbye. Una gasped at the awfulness of this separation during such uncertain times. Then the couple went on alone to Portsmouth, boarding the *Empress of Australia* for their Atlantic crossing.

Abel became absorbed with Una's demeanour as she sat on the edge of the tractor seat—she had finally agreed to using his tractor—and cut the engine to listen to daily chronicles of the sailing.

On the day it was announced that heavy ice was hindering the liner's advancement, she hardly spoke when they broke for bread. Then came reports of a gale tossing the flotilla about, followed by treacherous fog, separating the *Empress* from her naval escort vessels. It was said that the captain could smell icebergs in the air as the ship, taking the quicker but unforgiving northerly route of the Atlantic, passed the same area where the *Titanic* had gone down.

"And we thought we had it bad!" Una used her face covering to wipe dirt from her eyes.

It was beyond Abel how she bore no resentment for all these years when no help was offered by government. Although—notwithstanding his irritation over the whole ridiculous affair—it was true the king and queen's journey had gotten interesting for a while. At one point during the stormy voyage, he half-thought the flotilla

Spring, 1939

wouldn't make it. In the midst of the drama, he forgot his backache, neglecting also to notice a swollen finger, bruised blue-black and tender to the touch, possibly fractured.

In the evenings, he shovelled dust from his own acres by lantern light, getting maybe three hours' sleep before rising to help seed. But he did not feel tired.

Soon enough it was reported that the *Empress* had navigated the ice masses. The weather settled, and the ship made it to open waters and was sailing toward Quebec.

The king and queen's arrival had been delayed by two days. Several stops on the visit would have to be cut or shortened. But they had not struck an iceberg. Or been torpedoed.

That day, it was just Abel and Una out in the field. Crouching to smooth the soil within each furrow, and gathering pebbles.

"Goodness, they're brave," Una said. "Beginning their journey under such circumstances. Leaving everything they love behind to come to a place where they know they're despised. At least by some."

She stood and assessed their work. They had cleaned up the cropland as best they could, and finished reseeding. She picked up the radio and slipped her arm through Abel's, natural as could be, and walked with him back to the farmhouse.

Lewis Lyte came barrelling down the road, a coil of dust rising behind him. Pulling up at the door, he stepped out of his RCMP vehicle with a salute. "Howdy! Just on my way back from protocol training." He took the radio from Una, handed it to Abel and filled Una's arms with provisions. Reaching back into the car, he pulled out bags of coal, and wood, which he stacked against the side of the house.

"What's all this, Lewis?" Una peered into the bags.

"How about you take a break." He kissed her on the cheek.

Did she blush then, or was she flushed from their work in the fields?

"I suppose we could all use some coffee." She turned to Abel. "Would you?"

[153]

Lewis held the door open for her, then ducked inside himself, greeting Toby and Merle with a jovial nod. Once he had plunked his hat onto Toby's head and handed him a bar of chocolate, he told them about the gold.

According to Lewis, a rumour was circulating among the Mounties that the two destroyer ships accompanying the *Empress* were carrying 3,550 gold bars from the coffers of the Bank of England in steel boxes, stowed away in the ammunition rooms below the main decks, which would remain in the Dominion in case it was needed to fund a world war.

Lewis always told far-fetched stories.

While the Wisharts *oohed* and *aahed*, Abel poured coffee and speculated whether this was a fabrication deliberately spread by officials to boost the significance of Canada's role as an ally. Or could the tale be true? It would account for the flotilla's slow progress. It could have been seized by Germans. What was England thinking, undertaking such a precarious mission?

He hoped Lewis would go after gulping down his coffee. But Lewis didn't seem to be in any rush. He went over to the bags on the counter, pulling out flags, whirligigs and bunting. "Who's game for hanging decorations?"

Toby raised his arm. "Me!"

"Why so glum, Dodds?" Lewis gave Abel an elbow nudge. "You're not going to give us trouble, are you?" He returned his attention to Toby and Una, the three of them discussing the proper way to address royalty, while Merle observed from his rocker, blowing O-rings.

Abel took his leave.

Once home, he shovelled more dust. Every so often he stopped and looked through his binoculars, toward Grayley's station. They had all walked over there. Setting aside his uniform coat and rolling up his sleeves, Lewis got busy scrubbing the wood exterior with a bucket of water and a brush, sloshing most of the water onto the platform with his vigorous movements. Then he stopped to take off his shirt. Merle swept sand from the rail line, and Una hung bunting with Toby, glancing at Lewis as she tied her string to a sconce bracket, and turning away when he turned toward her.

In the lead-up to the king and queen's landing in Quebec City, Abel awaited news of unrest. Surely their majesties would not be well received by French Canadians. He scanned headlines of the latest *Tribune* dropped off by Cy, but found little of note.

An entire page was devoted to the queen's wardrobe—since her visit to Paris, she had transformed herself from a frumpy dresser to a fashion icon. Travelling to North America, she would have to be prepared for all eventualities, from the cold of the Rockies to muggy garden parties in Washington. She would need smart suits and gowns and rubber boots. The queen's clothing, it seemed, was of utmost importance.

Another page reported on the royal couple's entourage during their trip through North America. The king and queen each had a bodyguard. There was a private secretary, and ladies and a lord in waiting. A doctor, a hairdresser, a clothes dresser, footmen and others—sixteen helpers in total.

At the bottom left corner of the page was a short article concerning the MS *St. Louis*. On May 13, while King George and Queen Elizabeth were sailing to Canada, the *St. Louis* left Hamburg. Also crossing the Atlantic Ocean, the liner was headed for Cuba, and carried nine hundred and some German Jewish refugees. Surrounding this piece were columns discussing banquet menus, the colour of the king's official dispatch cases, particulars of invitation cards and procedures for parking large numbers of cars, and Mackenzie King's complaints of fatigue and sciatica.

Crumpling the pages, Abel tossed them into the stove and stoked the fire.

Heading out to see the Peloquins with Tansy, he thought about all that gold. Fifty tonnes, Lewis had said. While they ate dust.

Near their caboose, Lucie and Cyril's children worked in the garden, scooping sand into holes, wiping leaves clean with their small hands.

Through the open door, Abel heard crowds roaring. The Peloquins had their radio on loud. He left Tansy with the little ones and stopped to listen at the doorway steps. *The Quebec crowds are jubilant! This is a moment in history, folks. In Wolfe's Cove the king and queen were wholeheartedly welcomed, along with the prime minister and governor general, and a contingent of Huron-Wendat. Thousands upon thousands went wild. Later, on the Plains of Abraham, they were presented with a bouquet of English roses and French lily of the valley, and a chorus of forty thousand children sang "O Canada." The frenzy is extraordinary, we have never witnessed anything like this. At the day's close, the couple will sleep in the Citadel. Over the next month, Mackenzie King will accompany them everywhere.*

Cheers drowned out the reporter's voice. Abel could make out people crying, laughing, rejoicing. He thought about how the king and queen were spending their first night in a fortress that had been controlled by the British since they'd conquered New France almost two hundred years ago.

"D'une rare beauté, cette reine," he heard Cy say. "And that George, you know, he spoke not too bad."

Abel took off his hat and climbed aboard. His friends sat at their small table. Cy reddened when he saw him, turned off the radio and sprang to his feet, motioning for Abel to follow him outside.

"N-not you too." Abel pointed back at the railcar. "What happened— to your people having no loyalty to Britain?"

"Elizabeth makes an effort." Cy put a fist to his chest. "She spoke French! Ottawa makes no effort."

"I think we should c-c-confront them."

Cy watched his children. Two sat on Tansy's back, while the others cleaned leaves. "I got too much to lose here."

"What about the in-injustices you've endured?"

"Each one of us here got it hard." Cy appraised the surrounding wasteland. "But I don't know that vengeance'll fix wrongdoings."

He returned to the railcar, climbed the steps and called over his shoulder before disappearing inside. "You know they made special alcohol for this visit? *Crown Royal*. We oughta get some."

Lucie then appeared against the narrow metal door.

Abel looked up to her. "Surely you don't support this cir-circus?"

"We have a long history." She eyed his waist. "Let's see that cut." She came down the steps and pulled up his shirt, and seemed satisfied at how things were healing. Ushering her children out of the way, she then checked Tansy's legs. She patted Abel's horse and gestured toward his farm. "Una told me what she aims to do. You going to spruce up that barn of yours?"

"Don't know."

"You should take her to the movies."

"What— movies?"

"Tour newsreels."

"I've got no— time for that."

Lucie kept her gaze on him. "Wait too long and both your lives'll be on the wing. Like swallows."

Cy poked his head out then. "Qu'est-ce-que tu racontes?"

"Anyone can see it." Lucie turned her attention to her children, making sand castles in the garden. "Anyone can see what's about to happen. Here and over the ocean."

Pay no mind. I am not alone.
I have the sun and memories
of rain. On the radio
my parents sing of happy days.
—A.D.

16

The rosehip jelly glowed a rich, vibrant red on the kitchen table, like a beating heart against the scuffed pine. It was the last jar from the batches his father had made each year. And today, on his birthday, Abel would eat it.

He had baked bread the night before. Warming the loaf, he made coffee and fried some eggs. The funny thing about the jelly, he always thought, was that it didn't taste like roses. The sweetness contained a tartness, unanticipated and pleasing. Finishing his meal, he grilled two more pieces of toast, and brought them out to Elizabeth Moon and Tansy.

As if by miracle, sections of his winter wheat now grew in strips the sand seemed to have missed. As though his crop arrangement, perpendicular to the direction of the storm, had been partially shielded from the sand as it blew over. His Fairway grass started to sprout too. He had not scrutinized his rows closely after the dust storm. He couldn't bear to. He walked these patches of intact land, digging up a few plants to test survival before seedlings were apparent, leaving the root ball intact. Later in the day he'd bring them inside and spread them on the sill, where the sun could reach them. After a week, he'd wash off the soil and check for new growth. If the plants had white roots, they were healthy. Black roots meant the plants were dead, leaving little hope for a profitable crop.

Setting his samples aside in a burlap bag, he got down on all fours and dug for his father's gold, despite the growing sense that he wouldn't find any. Gold was for kings and queens and royal ships. Gold was for war.

He looked up when he heard singing. Toby wandered over, gas mask pulled back on his forehead. Wiping his hands, Abel stayed on his knees so that he was eye level with the boy. "How's your— breathing?"

"My Aunt Brynn's a nurse now."

"So I heard."

"She writes letters and sends toys. Says I pro'bly grew out of the dust sickness."

"Is that— possible?"

"Mom says anything's possible." He cocked his head. "Isabelle and Antoine said their parents say you're heartsick. How come?"

Abel stood. "Go home."

"Guess what?" Toby squinted into the sun. "The king and queen got bombed."

"Wh-what? When?"

Toby kicked at the dirt, ankles visible beneath the hem of the pants he had outgrown. "At dessert time. They got a cake bomb covered in chocolate. Invented just for them." He sighed. "I wonder. If the king's hand will get maimed with handshaking."

"Where did you learn that— word?"

"The *Tribune* says the king's brother Edward's hand got maimed, when he came here as a prince. From too much handshaking." His expression remained serious. "Lewis says the touring cars'll be bullet proof. With a secret dressing table compartment for the queen,

Spring, 1939

and space enough for King George to wear his feather hats while standing."

Abel gathered his shovel, trowel and bag of samples.

"Did you hear about the Ontario lookalikes?" Toby walked over to the axe a few yards away. "They offered to take their majesties' places so they don't get tired. And guess what else," he called over his shoulder. "Lewis says he'll make sure the king stops by." He pointed to the axe. "Why's this here?"

"It's stuck. Don't b-bother."

Toby struggled with the handle and then pulled the axe from the earth. Its blade shone in the sunlight as he trotted over, offering it to Abel.

"I t-tried my damnedest—" Abel stood before the boy, dumbfounded. "Never mind. Keep it. You earned it."

Toby smiled, front tooth missing. "You find gold yet?" He tucked the axe handle under his arm.

"Who says I'm— looking for gold?"

"Boppa told us. Mom and Lucie were laughing at your digging. Lucie says all you'll find is arrowheads and buffalo bones. I could help."

"I don't— need help."

"If I find gold can I keep it?"

"No."

"Never even got my commem'rative coin." After a few whacks to the soil with the axe, Toby looked up at Abel. "How come no one brought our free coins?"

"Because there's— no school here anymore."

"Is too." He brandished the axe at the silt-laden building.

"It's d-decommissioned."

"It's still there." Toby swung the axe through the air, making figure eights.

Abel pointed to the Wishart farmstead. "Scram."

The boy pulled his mask back down over his face and walked off in the direction of his farm. In Toby's slow march and occasional stumble beneath the sun, Abel saw himself as he was long ago. Shoulders slumped, head filled with worries that no one could allay.

After bringing his plants into the house and spreading them along the sill, Abel focused his binoculars on Toby running to his mother, performing some kind of dance.

She waved him off but he persisted, hopping and twirling with his axe until she took it away. Eventually she stopped her work, hands on hips. Her pants were enormous. Like the bloomers of a clown. She wore a headscarf to keep her hair back, but strands still blew in her face. Her son in his gas mask kept dancing, and for a moment Una danced with him. Then he wandered off and she returned to her weeding.

The way she wavered at the end of each row was comforting, like hands above a piano, taking a breath before the next movement. Not that Abel knew much about pianos or movements. Or music of any kind. But he remembered when Miss Kitty brought a wind-up gramophone to class, and kept it there a week, playing records for them. The most stirring melodies came from the German composers. Bach. Beethoven. Brahms. Head on her desk, Una's shoulders rose and fell as they listened to one melody. "Moonlight Sonata" or some such.

On your birthday, always do one thing to make yourself happy, his father once told him. What made him happy was seeing Una Wishart happy. Reaching for a packet of seeds in the cupboard, he headed outside again to cut back weeds around the barn. He had to use a scythe they were so thick. Adding topsoil to smooth the area out, he dug small holes here and there before scattering the seeds all the way around the dilapidated structure. It took him the rest of the morning.

Next he opened the barn door wide to air it out.

Covering his mouth with a bandana, he put on gloves and began clearing out the piled-up items. The decisions about what to keep or toss weren't easy. What could be sold for scrap? What could be

Spring, 1939

salvaged? A voice in his head said, get rid of it all. Burn it to the ground. Imagine the heat from such a fire.

First he removed feeding dishes and hay bins. He hauled broken implements out behind the barn, to the scrap heap he had going there, adding his father's old harrow, a cattle oiler, handleless shears and bladeless hoes. All this, along with other pipes and parts, he dragged to the back field, hidden from view.

With a wheelbarrow he cleared out evidence of stock — to think they once had a dozen cows — shovelling and disposing of mouldy dung. Sprinkling lime on the floor to cut the smell. Shovelling, shovelling.

He even fixed the broken ladder. Climbing into the hayloft with his broom, he swept away cobwebs and cleared ledges of bird droppings and mice nests.

The resident swallows had not yet found their way back in. He knocked down as many of the old nests as he could reach. They fell to the ground and cracked open, revealing dried grass and feathers.

He climbed down and assessed his work. Broken panes still needed replacing. He should also rake out the floor and spread wood chips. The barn door still stuck and the exterior needed painting, or at least a wash. But he could sort that later. He sat on a bale as the sun went down. The barn grew cold and dim.

In the morning he decided to bring Una what was left of the jelly. Maybe it wasn't a bad idea, like Lucie suggested, to invite her to see the newsreels. He was halfway across the plain, nearing the schoolhouse, when Lewis sped past with a honk, pulling up at the Wisharts'. Abel pretended to be headed for the school instead, and once inside, he waited by the Dutch door for Lewis to leave. But the RCMP vehicle stayed in front of the farmhouse.

The movies would be for another time. Leaving the jar on the teacher's desk, Abel returned home.

For a while he sat in his father's rocker, thinking. Then he retrieved the family tableware from the Hoosier cabinet, each piece of cutlery inside the box tarnished a dull grey-black.

After some porridge, he got going on the serving dishes and candlesticks, along with the mantel clock that had long ago stopped ticking. He remembered his father doing this yearly, soaking everything in a baking soda and vinegar mix, rubbing each item with a soft cloth.

Seeing the silvery surfaces reappearing, he wished he had kept up his father's tradition of polishing. He would have had something pretty to look at through the cabinet doors while the county turned to dust. Reflected in a water jug, even his own face didn't look so bad, his blemishes invisible on the metal.

After months of tinkering around with crude jury-rigged parts, he'd finally managed to repair the old family truck. Packing the valuables into a crate, he filled the truck with the last of Cy's gasoline. It started up after a few tries. Driving around to the back of the barn, he added what he could from the scrap heap to the truck bed, then drove to Sterling.

The number of uniformed men had increased in the city. Everyone seemed in a hurry. The soup kitchen was boarded up. The clerk in the trading post examined his possessions with a weary look, eyes glazed over. As if he had seen too many hard-up men that day already, and had no use for worthless relics.

At the Feed and Seed, Abel enquired about a generator and electric milkhouse heaters that could warm up a barn. A whole workshop of them had been seized from farmers in debt and were now being rented or sold. Choosing one of the older models that he was familiar with, Abel laughed, realizing it may have been his father's.

At the hardware store he bought a new axe. At the filling station he bought a barrel of gasoline. At a diner he ate a roast beef sandwich and a piece of cherry pie, and wondered if this was the place Una had sat when she almost ran away. But he couldn't find any art gallery, and guessed that, like many other businesses, it had closed.

Spring, 1939

At the Hudson's Bay he asked after a gramophone. He wanted a wind-up one that could be played anywhere. Even out in a field without electricity. The saleslady had only one of the early models left. Pulling a record from its sleeve, she provided a demonstration—a tune on saxophone and drums. "Have you got music?"

Abel shook his head.

She lowered her eyeglasses on her nose. "What's the occasion?"

"Barn dance."

"Jazz is popular these days."

"What about B-Beethoven?"

She raised an eyebrow. "For a dance?"

He counted his remaining dollars, holding on to a few coins before showing her what he had. She told him it was enough for a mix and made the selection for him. Then he went to the movies, parking where he could pay an old drifter to watch the truck.

"No war stories today," the girl at the wicket told him, and he said that was fine.

Inside it was all couples—a lot of them up to no good. All likely involved in illicit romances, Abel figured, and looking to escape their lives. The theatre was dank and smoky, smelling like parlour beer and sweat. He was glad he hadn't listened to Lucie. This was no place for a date—although everyone was so engrossed in the footage of the Royal Tour that no one seemed to notice the dismal surroundings.

Showgoers hooted and whistled at the palace on wheels, as King George and Queen Elizabeth, shadowed by Mackenzie King, waved at hundreds of thousands lining the railways and gathering at city events.

In Montreal they were greeted by some fifty thousand children waving flags and singing. Then they arrived in the nation's capital, making their way through a sea of onlookers to the unveiling of the Great War memorial.

The monument was granite, with bronze figures at the base representing the people of Canada who heeded the call to service.

Atop a stone arch, the narrator said, were the allegorical figures of Peace and Freedom. The tribute was named *The Response*.

Trumpets played and the crowd sang "God Save the King" and "O Canada." The tone of King George's speech was confident, his stutter subtle. When the ceremony ended, the king and queen strolled through the crowds, shocking the commentator. But they did as they pleased, their security details struggling to keep them within sight.

They mingled and seemed at ease. The queen said, "Hello, bonjour." Photographers snapped pictures. The king shook hands, said, "God bless." People cheered. Veterans wept. Then the royal couple said goodbye and moved on to their next destination.

Abel glanced around the movie hall.

In the half light, on the faces of those watching the large screen, he saw something he hadn't seen in a long while. An expression he recalled from a time before the worst times. When living was manageable, necessities such as food and homes were affordable, work was plentiful and the weather did not instill fear. The only word he could think of for the look was *contentment*.

It seemed to Abel that the whole population was under a spell. Forgetting their grim situation as they applauded the king and queen. Everyone in the theatre suspended disbelief until the reel ended, the projector stopped and the lights came on.

Above you tonight, a cup
dripping gold touched the sky's
dark table, leaving a ring mark.
—*A.D.*

17

As the train made its way east to west, rain preceded or followed. Farmers started calling the king George the Rainmaker. Often the sun's rays appeared through the clouds as if by divine intervention, just as George and Elizabeth stepped out from their carriage—a phenomenon people named king's weather.

It seemed to Abel that the whole goodwill tour was unbelievable, like a staged production. How was it that the same rail line that had transported tens of thousands of hungry, unemployed transients and protestors atop boxcars now carried the royal party in a gleaming train painted a rich deep blue with silver accents, adorned with imperial crowns?

He could hear, in the lighthearted voices on the radio, how even critical journalists were won over. Reporters described George and Elizabeth as down-to-earth and natural. Dignified but not too grand. The queen let people hug and kiss her. The king indulged anyone wishing to converse.

Then there were the onlookers. By the sounds of it, all of Canada turned up to witness the train go by, or to participate in welcoming parties. Throngs stretched for miles along the rail line between the train's preordained stops. Cities held weeklong celebrations. Traffic jams formed along busy roadways. If the engineer on the locomotive saw crowds ahead, he notified their majesties by pushing a buzzer, giving them time to make their way to the rear platform as the train slowed. Appearing in the doorway of the last carriage, they waved.

Apparently, this leisurely roll-by was enough to elicit widespread devotion.

Rural communities pooled the last of their coins to travel from various directions on different train lines, or by automobile, truck or tractor, buggy, horse or foot. Dressed in new homemade clothes, washed coveralls and brushed ten-gallon hats, people convened in cities and their outskirts, waiting on rooftops and in trees, standing on stilts and fences, climbing hills, settling in ditches, or in boats along rivers. Even hospital patients were wheeled out, waiting hours for a fleeting look, as if such a vision would heal them. Mackenzie King proclaimed that the visit was an end to hard times.

Abel stared out at the soil drift, willing rain. But Grayley stayed bone dry.

He waited for news of picketing and demonstrations. Stories of protestors gathering to disrupt public events, calling for social change. But it seemed no one objected anymore — that those wanting to air their grievances against the prime minister, or oppose the monarchy, were appeased.

He switched off the radio and returned to the kitchen window.

The country was charmed by the king and queen, just as Una was captivated by Lewis. Abel could see, from where he stood at the sink, how the logs atop the Wisharts' woodpile were near gone. Logs Lewis had brought that burned too quick, like the coal he dropped off, in the smallest of sacks.

All morning Abel tore pieces off the roof.

While he did so, he thought how his physical landscape — the only one he had ever known—was receding. Disappearing room by room, into a memory the plains would eventually swallow. Yet this economy of existence drew him closer to the sun, cleared his head and helped him to breathe more easily.

In the afternoon he brought the hand-held radio—a luxury his father had bought in the late twenties—out to the barn. The radio was clunky, with a rusted casing and a tinny tone compared to the Wisharts' new model, but it was functional. As he worked on flattening the dirt floor, he awaited real news. Hitler and Mussolini had just signed a strategic alliance. But he heard no reports on the Pact of Steel. Only vivid descriptions of military bands in ceremonial uniform, marching to regimental tunes in their majesties' honour, and anecdotes about the couple walking muddy streets and visiting stockyards, refineries and northern, off-the-track towns. Laying cornerstones and officiating openings, recitals and softball tournaments.

He was listening to an explanation about the royal coat of arms and the monogram of King George VI when Una arrived hand in hand with her son. "Jeepers, Toby. Look at what Abel has done! No wonder we've seen so little of him."

The boy ran off to climb hay bales. Abel turned off the radio.

"This tour is really something. I can't decide my favourite moment so far," she said as the voices died out. "Their walkabout at the war memorial was so moving, don't you think? Elizabeth has such a natural way of conversing. Did you hear what she said, when asked if she was Scottish or British?" Una pressed her hand against her heart. "She said, 'Since I've arrived in Quebec, I am Canadian.' And did you hear about their meeting the Dionne quints? Oh! And that uplifting reunion with the Ojibwe Chief, who served as the Prince of Wales' guide all those years ago. How old he was! He knew and remembered so much." She called out to Toby. "Should I tell him your favourite part?"

Toby was watching a swallow dart around in search of its nest. He nodded.

"It was the broadcast of his speech delivered in Winnipeg, aimed at the young people of the Empire. What did George tell you to do?"

The boy kept his eyes on the swallow. "Hold fast to all that's just and good."

"That's right." She entwined her fingers. "And what a voice! Everything he says is so rich and suspenseful. Wouldn't you say?"

Abel had to admit, he was impressed that the king's stutter had subsided. He would grant her this. "He does have— good articulation."

"I suppose my favourite moment"—her eyes followed the swallow now too—"is just listening for the hush every time they're about to appear. Just as they come out. That moment of a collectively held breath before the great roar."

He proposed she go to Calgary, where there would be fireworks, a bandstand show and street dancing till dawn.

"Oh, I don't care about those overblown events." She leaned against the barn door as the bird flew away. "Besides. It wouldn't be the same as welcoming them here."

Tansy whinnied for attention.

"Can I go see her?" Toby asked.

"Five minutes," Una said. "Then home."

He skipped toward the stable. "Won't be long before they reach Cutland County." She considered her frayed pants with holes in the knees. "If they're to be in Calgary on the twenty-sixth, they'll likely pass through Grayley tomorrow. I just wish..."

He knew what she was thinking. That the replanting had eaten away at their time, providing no opportunity to put together any real celebration. There hadn't even been time to wash or mend their clothes.

"Doesn't anyone c-care about anything else anymore?"

"Of course." She looked out at the station. "But there's nothing we can do about world events right now."

"You act as if— they're your friends."

Spring, 1939

"What of it?"

"You know n-nothing about them."

She crossed her arms and faced him. "I know that George likes to hop off the train to film wildlife with his camera. And that Elizabeth's favourite part of the day is telephoning the princesses. I know they're not crazy about North American cocktails. And that they like getting off the train in the middle of nowhere to stretch their legs, and race each other." Her cheeks went blotchy. "I know they're bolstering everyone's spirits. That the days feel less backbreaking because of them. And that's something."

Abel gritted his teeth. "Did you know, in — places where it doesn't rain, their outfits are sprinkled with water so they don't g-gather dust? That cities are — emptying their coffers for their entertainment?"

"That's a spiteful thing to say."

"This is a — ploy. For the prime minister to win favour. Once it's — over, you'll see nothing's changed."

"I disagree. I think everything will have changed." She turned to the barn, throwing her arms up in the air. "And what about all this?"

"This — is for you. Not them."

"How kind. I should never have bothered you with our trivial do."

"I only meant — "

She called out to Toby, who was practising his curtseys and bows in the yard. He ran to her and she kissed his cheek. "You're sticky." She took his hand. "You'll need a bath tonight."

She and Toby walked in the direction of the station, where Merle was finishing up the whitewashing. Lewis was there too. He seemed to be around a lot now, saving the day.

With their paintbrushes, they went over the cracked wood boards in the waiting area. Above the grey-brown land, clouds turned pinkish in the fading light. One looked like a fox. One like popped corn. And one a goblet.

Later, when Lewis had gone, the Wisharts moved on to the schoolhouse. Abel worried that they would spot what he had torn down. But they took no notice, or maybe they were indifferent.

He spooned his boiled wheat, letting it drop back into his bowl as he watched them walk home in the evening twilight of indigo hues. They walked ever so slowly. Merle put an arm around the boy, and Una held her shawl tight as she looked up at the sky.

He decided to exercise Tansy, the air too mild to not take advantage. Tying his horse outside the schoolhouse, he lit a lantern and went in to find the place swept clean, his father's jar of rosehip jelly gone. Grass garlands criss-crossed the room. They had dusted down the royal portrait. On the board in careful, cursive hand was written *Welcome Your Majesties*. In smaller letters—less carefully, as though in afterthought—*And Welcome Prime Minister Mackenzie King*.

The tour map had come unpinned and lay on the ground like a cast-off mantle. The king stared Abel down. Finding tacks in the janitor's toolbox, he refastened the map to the wall, running his finger over Grayley's rosehip.

He pulled the pieces of the pig from his coat pocket. He got the glue from the utility cupboard, dipped a matchstick into the container and pasted the wings onto the pig's back.

Waiting for the glue to dry, he glanced at the clock. The hands had not moved, it was still noon and midnight, no time had passed. The map fell again. Setting the pig on an apple crate, he fixed the drawing back in place, using the remainder of the glue to adhere it permanently to the wall.

Then he sat out on the front steps awhile. The Wisharts' house was surrounded in darkness, one light flickering within. He suspected she was cleaning out the stove, scrubbing chipped cups and saucers, in case their majesties might have time to stop in for tea. Baking a pound cake, polishing cutlery, fanning out thin serviettes.

As he approached the farmstead with Tansy, there she was, washing windows. Then she held a dress up against herself. Pressing

Spring, 1939

the fabric to her cheek she twirled around before tossing it to her son, who wore a paper crown.

Not long after, she came out to pick weeds that grew in the sandy soil along the fence line. Goldenrod and thistle, probably. As her shadowy figure moved back inside carrying a bouquet, Abel felt a sense of regret, like when a poem left him before he had a chance to write it down. Tansy nudged his shoulder. He gave his horse a peppermint and led her home.

Together we pursued immortality
as their majesties rode past
all we had and all we lost.
—A.D.

18

On the day the Royal Train was to pass through, the cloudless sky was so smooth it looked ironed. Abel fed the animals and milked Elizabeth Moon. He collected eggs, took his time with breakfast and drank two cups of coffee. At the sound of horse harness bells and a fiddle, he stepped outside. The Peloquins were travelling the road to Grayley. With the children in the buckboard, Lucie held the lines while Cy tuned his instrument at her side. Waving at Abel, they continued on. Then the Wisharts passed in the distance, going the way of the railway line to town, Toby balancing on the steel rail, hopping along the ties, joining their neighbours at the station.

As he combed his fields for pests, Abel watched the small retinue on the platform. Thinking about what he ought to do.

He waited till midday, when the sun was at its peak, the sound of dry soil cracking in the air. Fetching water from the warmed barrel outside, he transferred a few inches into the tin tub in the kitchen. Crouching in the tub, he scrubbed himself clean, lathering the tallow soap Lucie had given him. He used the whole bar. Then he dried off with his towel, which had thinned to gauze, wiped the puddle at his feet and wrung the droplets back into the tub.

After stitching the tear Freddie Teel's blade had made in his mother's yellow blouse, he dressed. He fastened his father's suspenders onto his one good pair of pants, whose dark navy colour concealed stains. He wound his father's pocket watch, attaching the chain to a belt loop. He brushed his teeth with soda and gargled with Lucie's sage rinse, shaved, combed his hair and parted it sidewards.

He wiped down the porcelain pigs, taking care around the glued parts of the broken one. Running a fingernail along the grooves in the wing, he emptied leftover grains of salt and pepper from the snouts into his mouth, which increased his thirst and hunger. "We had a good life here once," he told the pigs, angling them so they could see outside.

Through the window, the Wisharts and the Peloquins partnered up and hooked arms, practising a dance. Abel polished his boots and brushed his hat, got Tansy from the paddock and stayed with her awhile. The barn was finally empty. The crops planted. In the end what else mattered?

He led his mare to the stable, where she and Elizabeth Moon could graze away from any commotion. He made sure they had extra hay.

As he walked along the roadside, a handful of grasshoppers leapt before him. A reminder that devastation would always be a few feet ahead, somewhere in view.

He felt dead tired climbing the platform steps. Merle, groomed and smooth-faced, gave him a salute. Toby and the Peloquin children wore their best vests and seed-bag dresses. Even Cy had slicked his hair back with pomade. Una came out from the waiting room then, wearing the trunk dress Lucie had chosen for her — a floor-length evening gown that clung to her silhouette.

Abel swallowed hard before he spoke. "That's a ni-ni— lovely dress."

"It smells like cod." She barely gave him a glance. "I didn't think you'd come."

"Who wouldn't want— to meet a king and queen."

Assisted by Lucie, the children finished hanging flags and bunting. Every time the wind carried a note of a train's hiss, chug or puff, they hurried to line up. But the sounds were unreliable. Imaginary. No train came.

Cy fiddled. When he sang, his children joined in. It was a French folk song about Napoleon III and his family. Lucie said he used it to teach the little ones the days of the week, the only variation to the lyrics being the first and last word in each refrain: *Monday morning, the emperor, his wife and the little prince came to my house, to shake my hand. As I was gone, the little prince said: "Since that's how it is, we'll come back on Tuesday,"* and so on, to Saturday to Sunday, to Never... *Sunday morning, the emperor, his wife and the little prince came to my house, to shake my hand. As I was gone, the little prince said: "Since that's how it is, we won't come back again."*

Merle squinted down the line. "Must be a delay."

The children grew bored and left the platform to play in the dirt. Their clothes got coated in dust. Then Toby pointed to red uniforms in the distance and an RCMP vehicle moving at a crawl along the line. "Mounties!" He turned to his mother. "Are they looking for coal?"

Abel and his friends walked down the track a few minutes until they reached the three men at the grain elevators.

The lead sergeant gave orders and examined the rails. One Mountie stayed in the Ford sedan while another peered into the two standing elevators before circulating around the fallen one.

"Hello, folks." The sergeant greeted them. "What happened here?"

Cy swore under his breath. "He think we knocked it down for fun?"

Lucie drew her husband back.

"Is something the matter?" Una asked.

The sergeant's gaze lingered on her. "You all need to clear off."

"We live here, fellas," Merle said.

"All the same. You'll have to remove yourselves." The Mountie eyed the Peloquins. "May I see your identification cards?"

Abel shook their hands. "We d-d— we're not used to carrying identification around here." He pointed to their farmsteads. "That's us."

Una hugged her arms against the late afternoon's growing cold. "Lewis Lyte patrols our parts."

"Where's Lewis?" Toby stood on his tiptoes, searching.

The Mountie glanced up from his clipboard. "Posted further east."

For once something had gone Abel's way. "Can we b-be of service?"

The sergeant gestured to his cohort to start blocking off the area while the other Mountie remained in the vehicle, observing.

"This is our home." Una's voice wavered. "We have just as much a right... as anyone. To see their majesties."

"Ma'am, we only ask that you keep away from the immediate area. And not come close to the track." The sergeant studied his notes and approached Merle. "There a culvert up ahead?"

"Yessir. Nothin' there but thistle."

He looked Merle up and down. "You serve?"

Merle nodded. "Africa."

The Mountie pencilled something in. "Any interest in standing guard?"

"What for?"

"To make sure no one plants explosives. We've got twenty more miles to verify."

Merle tapped a finger to his lips. "S'pose so."

Una's grandfather got into the vehicle with the uniformed men, and they drove west toward the small, concrete bridge.

Abel followed the others back to the platform, where they waited until sunset. When the children grew cold and hungry, Una and

Lucie brought out cocoa and sandwiches. Cy lit the wicks in the sconces, so that their little station glowed like a coneflower. Nearby, the Mounties patrolled with flashlights. You could hear them calling to one another, walking up and down the track.

The children curled up on the benches. Lucie pulled blankets from the buckboard, and Cy fiddled a quiet song. *À la claire fontaine m'en allant promener, j'ai trouvé l'eau si belle que je m'y suis baigné... il y a longtemps que je t'aime, jamais je ne t'oublierai.* It was a sad melody. Abel was struck by how serene Una looked then. Smiling with the Peloquins and comforting her son as his energy waned. Helping the children tie ribbon around bunches of wolf willow, brushing away strands of hair which had fallen from her upsweep.

He wished he could talk with her of Heaven. Of whether or not there was a God. He thought how all of life was like a train—how just as things got to feeling good, it sped up, with no going back to fine moments.

Then he came to his senses, remembering how everyone in the prairies had been forgotten. This visit could never make up for what they had endured these past years. He checked his father's pocket watch. It was nearing eleven p.m.

A dim orb of light appeared above the rail line, coming from the east.

Una leapt up, her gown rippling. "Here they come!"

The children waved their flags as the pilot train neared. Then the advance locomotive was upon them, creating a wind that rushed across their bodies, enveloping them in a cloud of dust. The engineer pulled on the horn. Abel could see inside the illuminated cars. Journalists looked down, busy at their work. Within seconds the station platform was once more engulfed in darkness, the flames in the sconces faltering and going out.

"It won't be long." Una took the box of matches from the bench and relit the lamp wicks. "Their majesties will soon follow."

Amidst the excitement and fuss, Abel slipped away unnoticed.

Through his binoculars he watched the taillights of the Mounties' vehicle disappearing westward. Then he made his way to the culvert. How often had he walked up and down this line, fingers bleeding from picking coal, stomach empty? He knew every tie. Every crack in each plank of wood. He knew how oil stains and rust spots changed over time. And how the Horseshoe River once ran under the track, in forceful torrents.

When he reached Merle, the sky was dark as tar.

The old man hunched over his lantern, carving. "'Lo there, stranger. Just whittling a chess set for Toby." He held the bit of wood up so Abel could see. A knight.

Although the Mounties had already done so, Abel offered to look over the culvert again. He walked beneath the pass, feeling the concrete with his hands. Feeling only dried grass and sand. Tumbleweed and dust and the echo of water.

He sat with Merle. "Why not— join the others."

Merle shook his head. "Can't have you sufferin' alone."

"I'm happy to— do this."

"I am feeling a bit stiff," Merle finally agreed. "If you're sure."

Abel nodded.

Merle rose. "You don't want to partake." He shoved his knife and knight into his pocket. "Yet here you are, all gussied up. Hat reshaped and clean. As though you were headed to your own funeral."

"I'm not in the m-mood for merriment."

Merle undid the top buttons of his shirt and pulled at the collar to loosen it. When he turned to face Abel, a dark line crossed his neck, like the shadow of a rope. "I ain't one to stop a man from doing what he feels he's meant to do. But some cattle bandits you can't catch. Best to let 'em go."

He plodded off into the darkness.

Once his neighbour was out of view, Abel stepped back into the dead grass and waited, refocusing his binoculars on the station,

Spring, 1939

trying to grasp Merle's meaning. He had just minutes to sort through his thoughts then he saw Una, and only Una, on the platform. Graced by the diffuse light of the sconces. Una Maeve Wishart in her crocus-coloured gown, waiting for something to believe in, for something that would raise everyone's spirits.

She paced and peered into the blackness. As if she could not take much more disappointment. As if one more blow would cause her to collapse like the grain elevator.

The Royal Train's headlight came into view like the large eye of a smoke-breathing beast.

To serve someone. What did it mean? All Abel wanted was what she wanted. If he could just stretch out their time together. Make sure she suffered no more losses. If he could just get the prime minister's attention. Make him see how they barely survived.

Merle appeared on the platform. There was no way he could see Abel. Yet he faced him, shoulders squared, raising his right hand and holding it open in a gesture that said, I am here. Or farewell.

Both families rushed forward and lined up. The boys removed their caps. The girls picked up their bouquets. Una pinched her cheeks, smoothed her dress and licked a hand to wipe down Toby's hair. She had promised this arrival since winter. Yes, they were late, but they had come. The king and queen had come to Grayley. Just as she'd said they would.

As the train neared, everyone stood at attention. Even Cy kept poised, bow raised above fiddle, ready to play. Here it was. Their held collective breath.

Abel waited for the familiar sound of brakes. He would give his friends their moment. With discretion, he would then approach and ask to have a word. He would not ruin anyone's joy.

In the quiet of the late night, the engineer didn't blow the whistle.

Puffs of steam dissipated in the air above the headlight. Any second, their majesties would come out from the back carriage door. Abel couldn't see from where he was positioned, but he imagined the king and queen stepping out and greeting Una, her family and friends. At the very least the train would slow, and their majesties would wave and smile. Surely they had been given the signal that locals were waiting—had been waiting all day, all evening, all year, all their life—for an occasion such as this, to affirm that their existence mattered. But the train passed by the residents of Grayley without stopping or slowing. No prime minister or king or queen appeared.

Cy dropped his bow. Merle shook his head. Lucie crouched down to the children. As for Una, she peered down the track, wiping her cheeks. *Heartless,* Abel thought. *Mackenzie King is heartless.*

He threw down his binoculars and scrambled onto the track.

Within seconds he felt a barely perceptible rumbling beneath his feet. Pressing his boot down on the rail he felt a quivering as the light of the engine beamed nearer.

Fireworks went off. Or was it a flare gun fired by the engineer? There were so many sparks, the train a quarter-mile away, moving toward him at what—fifty, sixty miles per hour? Abel waved his arms, willing the engine to stop. Believing that it would stop. For her. That brakes would begin screeching.

The locomotive was going too fast, its thrust too powerful, or those on it did not care. And nothing he did—even in death—would change that. The Royal Train hissed and puffed and came at him, horn blaring, extinguishing his lantern as though his father were beside him saying, *It's over. Let go.*

He tumbled into the dry riverbed as the carriages ran over the culvert and away from Grayley.

After the train passed, Abel scrambled up the incline. Standing in the dust, he leaned forward, hands on his knees and caught his breath. Then he laughed. He laughed until it felt as though the stitches in his side had split open, only this time the cut didn't hurt.

*Hand in hand inside
the five petals
of the bristly wild rose.*
—A.D.

19

He took the back fields home, tripping and fumbling as he rushed along the uneven ground. Guided by the trench of light through the kitchen window from the bracket lamp he had left lit by accident. Once he reached the farm, he pulled open the barn door. Swept the space clean, dragged bales out for tables and removed sheets off the rented equipment he'd kept hidden until now, in case Harold Nettles came around.

Then he brushed Tansy and rode her back to the station, tying her next to Marmaduke. They were all still there. Like statuettes from a model train set. Cy and Merle smoked in silence. Lucie tidied up. The children played kick the can, and Una sat on the platform bench, waiting. Sitting next to her, Abel looked along the track to that dark place where he had stood a short time ago. The Mounties and their roadblocks were already gone.

"They'd have liked it here, I'll bet." She stared at her hands, rubbing her cracked skin. "Without all the fanfare. I thought they'd stop and chat... at least for a minute." She glanced at the children. "Toby is heartbroken."

"He'll— forget soon enough." Abel thought back to his own boyhood. "As soon as the next event rolls around the c-corner."

"Corner? What corner?" She laughed. "The plains have no corners. There's no turning anywhere here, except around ourselves."

"It was a— noble idea."

"You were right." Her dress flowed over her boots. "This isn't a personal visit. It's a political arrangement between countries."

Toby approached holding the king's letter, his eyes puffy. Una slipped it into her pocket. "They were in their berths." She squeezed his hand. "It's a long journey and they need rest. I'm sure if they knew we were here..."

Lucie approached. "It was a fine train though, wasn't it?"

"I liked the picture on the front," Toby said in a small voice, "with the lion and the unicorn."

Merle and Cy came over. "That's their coat of arms," Merle said.

"That your grand plan, then?" Cy pointed at Abel with his bow. "You tell 'em to keep on goin' outta here?"

Abel checked his father's pocket watch. It was past midnight. "How about— a dance. No p-point letting this spoil the night."

Lucie's mouth fell open. Cy let out a laugh. Merle's eyebrows arched, and Una's eyes widened. Even the children stared. As if such a proposition could never come from one such as him. As if they didn't quite trust his offer. One of the Peloquin girls tossed her bouquet onto the rails. The others followed, making a game of it.

"Bon ben." Lucie gave a clap. "On y va."

They put their teacups and saucers in a crate and packed up the cakes, pies and scones. Everyone piled into the Peloquins' cart—except Una, who mounted her own horse—and followed Abel, the group riding together to the farm beneath a moon that looked like a scythe.

His neighbours rushed into the barn, laying out food and drink on the bales. He'd strung up lights and had the milkhouse heaters on, powered by the generator. Choosing at random from the assortment of tunes, he wound up the gramophone, which was set up on a sawhorse, and jazzy swing filled the space. If he had to say so himself, it was a fete fit for a king and queen.

All night they danced, singing along to records and Cy's fiddle. All night Una smiled and laughed, like she had as a schoolgirl long ago.

Once in a while a swallow swept in, flitting above them. Abel wondered if the birds, in their steely resolve to rebuild their nests, were indeed a sign of good fortune.

At dawn she approached him by the sawhorse, where he changed records and watched her dance. A lemonade light spilled through the barn door. "Let's race." She caught her breath. "Like old times."

He felt himself redden and excused himself.

In the house he grabbed the best of his own food he could find, two small plates and cups, and a blanket, packing these into Tansy's saddlebag before returning to where she waited at the music table. "Alright," he said. "Let's go."

They left everyone eating pie.

A pale glow lit the prairie. They gave hay and water to Marmaduke and Tansy, and then mounted their horses and lined up at the pump. Once she brought down her arm they were off, galloping past the burnt church and community hall and boarded-up township, past the station and grain elevators, and then further.

They rode along the dry riverbed, following the ribbon of rail a mile then two, three, four, ten miles out, flying past lost years, Tansy moving so swiftly it was as if she had grown wings. Just as they reached that distant plain where the river course ended, the horses together slowed. And he saw roses. Wild roses as far as the eye could see. Of an abundance and a perfume like nothing Abel had ever experienced, the bushes so heavy with buds their thorny branches arched and drooped.

He couldn't understand. He had come this way recently and seen nothing. Not since before the drought—not since their youth—had there been anywhere close to this many blooms.

They dismounted to let the horses cool and rest.

Una sat on a flat river rock, taking it all in, while Abel led Tansy through a thicket where the flowers spread, or so it seemed, all the way to the horizon. Searching for an open spot, he unpacked the provisions from the saddlebag. Setting down his family quilt, he laid out their sunrise meal: white apples, cornbread, Elizabeth Moon's cheese and butter, and coffee.

"Keep guard," he told Tansy, and walked back through the growth of small trees.

When he reached Una she was looking west along the line. "Which train is that?" she pointed at railcars stopped up ahead.

He focused his binoculars. "It's— just a hauler."

"I heard nothing go by in the night. We'd have heard it."

"Could be a maintenance— crew."

She wanted to collect petals, wet with dew, for tea infusions and syrup, and to make candies. She held the front of her dress up like a basket. It took a while for her to gather what she needed. He helped pour the petals into her saddlebag before she passed with him back through the trees, leaving her horse by the empty riverbed.

When they emerged on the other side of the thicket, a couple was already there, sitting a ways up. *How can this be?* Abel thought. He was beyond tired, that was how. He rubbed his eyes. Opening them again the couple was still there. Probably drifters.

Una grabbed his wrist. She crouched, pulling him down with her. "It's them!" she whispered.

He looked through his binoculars. King George VI and Queen Elizabeth sat with legs outstretched, leaning back on their hands, among the pink blossoms. Nearby, the Mounties strolled and chatted without even their hats on, as though off duty.

Una reached for the viewing glasses and watched a good long

moment. Motioning for Abel to follow, she crawled nearer, until they could hear their majesties without being seen.

"Where are their—" Abel started to ask.

"Shh! Their attendants?" She handed him his binoculars. "On rambles, they often ask for privacy."

They wore what looked like regular tweeds. Aside from sunglasses, they were without adornment or costume. They didn't resemble their glamorous newsprint photos. Abel had never seen them so unencumbered. They looked like two ordinary people. Elizabeth lay back on her elbows. George yawned and said, "Mmmm." Bumblebees buzzed. The roses seemed to breathe and open further. The queen plucked one and twirled it between her fingers. "We haven't this variety at home," she said. "I wonder if we can get seeds."

"What are they called?" her husband asked. "Those little furry ones?"

"Gophers, Bertie. They're called gophers."

"What's that on his finger?" Abel whispered.

"A bandage," Una said in a low voice. "He crushed it in the carriage door in Saskatchewan."

Huddled close to Una, Abel could see the calluses on her hands. The eyelash on her cheek. The sunburn on her collarbone at the edge of her dress. He heard her every breath. Felt each one as his.

The queen smelled the rose and said, "Peppery." Then she sat up, kissed the king and leaned slightly forward. "This is the most beautiful place," she inhaled deeply, "that I have ever seen."

She rested her head on his shoulder, and her husband put his arm around her.

All at once Abel realized how foolish it was to blame his hardships on two human beings. *Let them keep their illusions*, he thought. *Let them not know our suffering.* Maybe they were pawns, too. Maybe George and Elizabeth felt as exhausted as everyone else. It seemed, just then, that they would rather sit in the dirt with nothing, for some quiet time together, than possess all the world's gold. How much control did they have, really, over the decisions of politicians and military leaders?

George let out a heavy sigh.

Elizabeth's shoulders slumped. "I suppose we must go."

He nodded, and they helped each other to stand.

By the time Abel caught sight of Tansy wandering over, it was too late. Una stifled a gasp as his mare went straight to the queen.

"Why, hello!" she said.

Tansy nuzzled Elizabeth.

"Where in the world did you come from?" George looked around.

The queen petted her. "I wish we could stay." Feeding Tansy something from her pocket, she murmured to her. All Abel made out was, "Adieu."

As the king and queen headed back, their security detail rejoined them, following close. Tansy stopped grazing to watch them. Nearing the train, they slowed as if they didn't want to get back on.

Abel stood with Una, hoping the royal couple would look back. Willing them to gaze one last time upon this magnificent place. But neither turned. Maybe they were trained to never look at a moment once it was over. To move only forward, because what other choice was there?

The prime minister rushed out of one of the railcars. The royal couple's staff encircled them, and Mackenzie King ushered them up the railcar steps. They boarded at the rear of the last carriage. Then the door closed after the trio like the door of a Black Forest cuckoo clock.

The locomotive pulled away. Continuing its journey westward, the train appeared to disappear into the ground, railcar by railcar, while smoke drifted into the sky like a smudge of lead.

Una made her way to the spot where the king and queen had been. Abel followed. The royals had left no trace.

Spring, 1939

"What did she say to you?" Abel petted Tansy where Elizabeth had just put her hand. "What did she give you to eat?"

Tansy blinked, swinging her tail. She would not betray the queen's confidence. He would never know what secrets were offered up to his horse.

Returning to the picnic blanket, Abel and Una ate cornbread and drank coffee without speaking. Tansy lifted her front leg every so often as she stood in place. Abel worried about her return home. They needed to go before the swelling started. He began gathering his dishes.

Una folded and rolled the quilt. She carried it in her arms through the thicket as if it were a luxury silk and not a worn old thing. When she handed it to him, he offered it back. To keep, in memory.

They returned to Grayley as slowly as the king and queen had returned to their duties, the sun on their backs, a gentle breeze blowing, swallows dancing overhead. Nearing town, they encountered one of the Mounties from the night before, collecting stray roadblocks. He was friendlier now that the night had passed without incident.

"We saw the train," Abel said. "Stationed up at the next siding stop."

The Mountie nodded. "We don't give much advance warning for the overnights. Security protocol."

"Why did they not park here?" Una asked.

"Up ahead was the planned service stop." He batted away some flies. "A crew was at the ready to divert both trains to a side track. We couldn't change it around just for you lot. Your boyfriend did try, though."

Una sat upright. "Pardon?"

"Lewis Lyte. Your beau."

"Oh, he's not..." She crinkled her nose. "Never mind. I just wish we had known. We could have brought them hot chocolate and sandwiches. They could have come and danced."

"You'd have seen nothing. They were asleep."

"Well." She stroked Marmaduke's neck. "We're sorry we missed them."

The Mountie tipped his hat. "Next time."

"Except," she said, "there won't be any next time."

"Not likely," the Mountie agreed. "At least not in our life."

When they reached the barn it was empty. Everything had been cleaned up and cleared out, and everyone had gone. It was as though nothing had ever happened there.

"If we told them..." Abel said.

"No one would believe us. I only wish Toby..." Una's thoughts trailed off. "She was radiant, wasn't she?" She smiled. "She seems so warm. And he seems so sincere. And shy." She hesitated, then reached out and touched Abel's cheek. Feeling her fingers on his skin, he couldn't move. "All these marks," she said. "I always thought it was because you had fallen in roses."

"Forgive me." Abel cleared his throat. "For how I treated you. When you came home."

She walked back out to her horse. "Oh, I don't give a fig." She picked a paper crown up off the ground. "I forgot about all that silliness long ago." She rubbed the crown with her fingers, taking out the creases before she looked up at him again. "To think. No one will ever know but us. That King George VI and Queen Elizabeth spent the night here." Lifting the quilt off the saddle, she brought it to her face and smelled it.

Someone whistled in the distance. Lewis was crossing the fields with Toby on his shoulders, both waving. He wore a white T-shirt and denim, his hair dishevelled. He was off duty, then.

"He's a bit of a nuisance," Una waved back. "But Toby adores him."

Abel put on his hat. "My workday should've begun hours ago."

She got onto her horse, tilted her head back and laughed. "You didn't even notice."

Spring, 1939

"Notice what?"

"You're speaking without... you're speaking freely."

Una waited for whatever he had to say. Anything. Tell her anything. Only now, he found, he could not utter a word.

She galloped off, a swath of purple dress glistening behind her. When she reached Toby and Lewis, she jumped off Marmaduke and helped her son on, and ambled with them back to the farmstead.

Una's figure waned in the morning light. After she disappeared, Abel turned homeward. In the stable, he greeted Elizabeth Moon with free-flowing words. In the henhouse he chatted with the chickens. In the fields he sang songs, testing, pushing, waiting for the usual disruptions and blocks. But none came.

All day he mused over how just hours before, he and Una had sat together, in a manner of speaking, with the king and queen of England. The king and queen, sitting on the ground of Cutland County, sharing a private moment. Here was something that could not be taken away. While he worked, he thought about the strangeness and magic of what had bloomed out there in the middle of the dry land.

Then it rained.

Summer 1939

> *In the event of war, meet me on the horizon at dawn.*
> —A.D.

20

Men fell from the sky. Airplanes flew overhead. By this time, Abel's wheat was plentiful. Spilling over footpaths he and his father made when he was a boy, so that when he went to investigate the falling men, he had to walk on his crop, crushing leaves and kernels.

The men were in training, parachuting onto the uncultivated plains surrounding his fields. From the house he watched them drift, as if from silk handkerchiefs tossed into the sky, spiders on a gentle breeze.

"Join us!" A paratrooper waved to him one day, while he was out combing for rust, examining the stems and heads of his plants for reddish-brown lesions. Abel waved back but held off fraternizing with them, returning instead to the house. Within a week, the airborne troops moved on. And he went back to concentrating on his labours, uninterrupted.

He had almost forgotten about this stage of the growing season, when feathery stems of varying shades of green grew from the earth, swaying in the breeze. It was his favourite period. How long had it been since he had walked the fields without dust blowing into his eyes?

After the king and queen passed through, Cutland County received just enough rain to replenish the sloughs and wells. Enough rain so that when he tried the yard pump, water trickled forth as if from a hidden spring. Enough rain to make the crops grow, gradual enough that no flooding occurred.

Pulling weeds, he looked for pests and disease but found none. In the distance he could see the Wisharts doing the same. Their crops had taken. Their strip tilling had worked. Lewis Lyte stopped by often. He fixed their Wincharger and got them an old truck. Everyone was busy. The Peloquins, too. No one visited Abel. He packed up the milkhouse heaters, generator and lights, returning them to the supply company. The gramophone and records, he kept.

The winter wheat grew well and quickly. Through July, his crops verged on maturity, strengthening in the sun, with the right amount of light rain at the right time. No extreme heat shrivelled the kernels. No windstorms tore the prairie apart. At night, between coyote calls, he heard the wheat crackling. In the daytime the stalks basked in the sunlight, pushing up with snaps and sighs.

His Fairway grass thrived too, rippling like the ocean the king and queen had departed on after winning the hearts of millions. Even Tansy and Elizabeth Moon were mesmerized by its movement, before they lowered their heads to graze.

For weeks he did not have to add water to stretch Elizabeth Moon's milk. He strained the milk and set it to rise, and the cream skimmed from the top of the pan was thick and flavourful. The butter churned from the cream melted on the tongue. The hens laid more eggs than ever. He bought a rooster, and chicks hatched. All summer, life was like a fairy tale. The sort of story in which everything greened and grew, after ten years of tribulation.

War stories also multiplied.

Evening news was overtaken with reports of escalating tensions. Britain continued trying to appease all sides. Russia could not

Summer, 1939

decide which side to take, Mussolini threatened battle, and Hitler was obsessed with Poland.

Abel decided not to listen anymore. Why immerse himself in speculation, why engage with countries' posturing and huffing? It was none of his concern. If war broke out, wheat demand would increase and prices would rise. Although there was an oversupply again in the global market, he wasn't worried. What he had in mind for next year was rapeseed, which produced an oil that stuck to wet metal. Rapeseed could be sold as a lubricant for naval ships and steam engines. If the world went to war, he would put his efforts into experimenting with new crops. If this second war lasted as long as the first, he would profit.

Every day he reached for his binoculars. Past the schoolhouse, the Wisharts' bountiful wheat grew. Often Una was out there, examining her plants, replanting the patches that hadn't taken root. Focusing on the grown-over path dividing their fields, Abel realized that the gold his father claimed to have planted — Happy Sanderson's trove he had searched for most of his adult life — was a made-up war story. It was just like his father to fabricate a grail quest to keep Abel going. Right here was the true precious commodity — his fields and the Wisharts' mixing with one another, crops turning from green to rich amber.

One morning in August, Harold Nettles' automobile glided down the road, passing Abel's farmstead and coming to a halt at his neighbours'. Both he and the Wisharts were in the same position. If harvest failed, they would have to sign their farms over. Harold had recently visited Abel to say that there would be no more agreements with the bank. Sizing up Abel's lush fields in the bright of day, he was taken aback. "Looks like your luck is changing." Abel said it had nothing to do with luck. When Abel told him about his plans for rapeseed, the banker offered to bump up his line of credit. That same morning, the Wisharts had driven off somewhere with Lewis.

Abel told Harold they weren't home, but even still the banker had pressed on and knocked at their door, waiting a good fifteen minutes in the yard.

Now he had returned, and pulled up near the barn, where Una and Merle stood. Abel focused his binoculars as Harold removed his hat and hung his head. To Abel's embarrassment, Una fell to her knees. He wanted to rush over, pull her up, and say, *Don't plead with him. You do not need to beg.* He wanted to shake some sense into that tactless little man, demand of him some decency.

Give them time, he thought. *Give them time to harvest.*

Merle went inside and came back out with his rifle, and Harold rushed back to his automobile with his unopened briefcase and drove away.

That afternoon, Abel visited the Wisharts. While Merle and Toby threw a ball back and forth in the yard, he walked hip-deep through the fields with Una.

She glanced over at his property. "You'll have a high yield this year."

"I guess the king's weather saved us."

"Harold says ours is looking too brown." She crushed some kernels between her fingers.

"The dark colour's no reason for concern."

"He thinks we're through. He's giving us thirty days' grace." She squinted southward. "Jake was right to stay away. He knew we'd fail." She laughed. "Lewis keeps urging us to take a room in the city. Imagine us cooped up like that! Brynn's the city girl. Not me. Toby would be like a caged animal, and poor grandad. He'd lose his marbles." The lines at the corners of her eyes deepened. "It's been such a long time since we've seen this. Like hammered gold. Almost seems a pity to cut it."

She had lost her pep. Abel thought back to the second half of the Royal Tour. By then you could see in newspaper photos how at each whistle stop — though Mackenzie King appeared energized — the king looked frail amid decorative arches adorned with flowers and flags. As for the queen, she maintained her trademark wave, but she too seemed to lose her sparkle. Especially once a third, secret guard train was added to the procession. Una said Lewis divulged that this had been necessary, due to rumours of German sympathizers and spies among the crowds. As the masses got bigger, hundreds of thousands of onlookers engulfing them, the king and queen seemed to wilt. Their weariness was evident in newsprint images. On the radio you could hear that the king's stutter had returned and worsened. Both sounded close to crying — from exhaustion or emotion, it was impossible to tell — as they gave their farewell address in Nova Scotia.

It was as though King George and Queen Elizabeth had assumed the burden of the country's poverty and misery, in an effort to provide people with a measure of joy.

Reporters' voices trembled describing the tour's end. Saying Canada had a unifying experience unparalleled in its history, and now had an intimate relationship with its sovereigns. Abel would never admit it, but as he listened to a live report of their vessel sailing away, surrounded by a fleet of Canadian warships, he was rapt. He had never in his life heard such cheering. Felt it in his marrow. In that moment something in him shifted. He no longer felt frustrated, or that the people of Cutland County had been abandoned. He felt ready to start over.

The wheat rustled like a waterfall. Una ran her hands through the heads and stems.

"Let's do your fields first," he said.

"But you've got to get to yours. Or it'll spoil."

"There's time for both."

He squeezed some kernels between his thumb and forefinger, and tasted. The crop was dead ripe. Ready for harvest. Without infernal heat or black blizzards, Una's plants had grown quickly. He gave her a few kernels to try.

She smelled the grain and bit into it. "Alright," she said. "It feels too soon, though."

Her headscarf was of the same shade and shine as the evening gown she'd worn to greet the king and queen. She had cut it up, dividing it into practical pieces. He wanted to ask if she had a patch to spare that he could keep. Instead he told her that he would ask the Peloquins if they could come and help gather in the yield, as they had in the past.

Tansy's coat had gone paler than snow and ghosts. Abel was ambling with his mare when a small military plane flew overhead. They both looked up. Through summer, fewer trains went by, and more planes appeared. Circling, diving, coasting out to the base near Sterling. Tansy wasn't keen on their whining. Abel, too, missed the low hum of locomotives.

He did mouth exercises as they walked. "Pretty plane on the plain practising possible positions," he repeated, each word pouring forth smooth as cream, though Tansy didn't seem to notice his improved delivery. Or she had something else on her mind. "What did the queen tell you?" he asked. But still his mare revealed nothing.

When they reached the railcar, he found his friends packing supplies. The children wrapped jars of preserves in clothing, which they arranged in bags and loaded into the buckboard, while Cy and Lucie filled vegetable crates in the garden.

Abel left Tansy with one of the twins, who gave her a carrot. "We'll be starting on the Wishart fields tomorrow," he told Lucie.

She put down her spade. "Why not yours first? Before the heads shatter?"

"We saw that criss de marde Nettles zoom by." Cy spat in the dirt. "That why you're rushin'?"

"Their grain's ready. I'm only helping a little."

"Sure, sure." Lucie led him into the caboose. "Just the usual neighbourly devotion."

The contents of their dwelling were packed up. Furniture, rolled straw mattresses and pots and pans were stacked in a corner, as if the Peloquins were setting out already for the season. Only the small table and chairs remained in place. Lucie poured cold tea. Cyril came in and swung the windows open. They sat in the warm cross-breeze.

Abel drummed his fingers on the table. "What's going on?"

Lucie ignored the question. "What are you dreaming of these days, Abel? Your features aren't as stern."

"Why haven't you married?" Cy added. "Things not workin' down below?"

"Why does it look like you're leaving?" Abel's throat went dry.

Cy rose and poured real drinks. "One for you, one for me, one for eternity."

They toasted.

"To peace." Lucie exchanged a look with her husband that said, *You tell him.*

Cy poured himself another before facing Abel. "Went on a ride the other day. Saw 'em putting up wire fencing. For camps."

Abel tried making sense of this. He was aware that jobless immigrants were being deported. Only British and Americans were allowed into the country anymore. The prime minister had also turned away the refugees aboard the MS *St. Louis*, refusing them safe harbour. This happened while the king and queen were in Washington, talking about the international situation with President Roosevelt, eating hot dogs from paper plates. Few had paid attention to the ship denied sanctuary, which had returned to Europe, where most of its passengers would likely perish under Hitler's regime. The Voyage of the Damned, they called it.

"Camps for who?" Abel tugged at his shirt cuff.

"Foreigners. Prisoners of war. This enemy or that." Cy shrugged. "People like us. Not to mention Lewis Lyte's always hanging around now."

"He's alright," Lucie said.

Cy lit his pipe. "I s'pose. But his comrades are goodfornothins."

"Don't go," Abel implored his friends.

Lucie reached for his hand. "We're not like you. Our memories aren't tied up here."

"This is your home."

Lucie looked outside. "Not anymore."

"Come live with me. At my farm."

Lucie shook her head. "It's not our place."

"Ask your other gal." Cy chuckled, and his wife smiled.

"You'll come back next spring?"

Neither spoke.

"Worry about yourself," Lucie finally said. "We're not destitute."

The Peloquins would never see themselves as dispossessed, Abel understood then. Wherever they went, they would be self-sufficient. Held up by each other.

A cargo train hurtled by. It was so loud, so close, that the caboose shook in the deafening roar. Abel wondered how they had endured it all these years.

After the train passed, Lucie spoke again. "I saw the queen that night."

Cy put his glass down. "Comment ça, you saw her?"

"She was awake. I saw her pull back the curtain from the sleeping car." She clasped and unclasped her hands. "I can't describe it. The moment the queen looked at me."

The three of them watched the cargo train vanish down the line. Lucie stood and observed her children through the open door, playing in the sun. "Her look was one of fear. Like she was trying to keep it tucked inside herself, for no one to see. Like she knew even her own little princesses will die someday. Like all of us. I think she felt my own fear too." She looked at Cyril. "After harvest we go." She then turned to Abel. "But you," she said. "Forget the world's darknesses. And think of love."

Soon there'll be a harvest
but no one to harvest.
Gilded fields spill forth as I
set forth and take your leave.
—A.D.

21

Abel fuelled the tractor, greased and readied the binder and drove out of the shed in the morning twilight beneath fading stars. After his own harvest, he'd finally be able to pay off the old machines, along with the rest of what was owing. By fall he would never have to see Harold Nettles' pudgy face again. Next year, if all went well, maybe he'd even buy one of those newfangled, all-in-one self-propelled units that did all the work for him, cutting, threshing and separating the kernels from the chaff.

The Peloquins were already at the Wisharts' when he got there, Lucie settling into the bunkhouse with her four youngest and Toby, while Cy and the three older children sharpened pitchforks and scythes with Merle, and readied the wagon and bins that would later transport the grain to the elevators. A long table made up of old doors and trestles was set up outside. Una brought out fried eggs, tomatoes and onions, and they breakfasted half-asleep as the sun rose deep copper, like a flattened penny on the track.

It was easy to settle into the harvesting routine. They had done it for so many years, both generous and lean, that it was embedded in their muscle memory. It was good to come together, knowing that the yield would again be abundant.

Una rode the tractor, pulling the binder through the fields behind it. Merle, Cy and his three and Abel walked alongside as the machine cut and bound the crop into bundles. When it got stuck, they untangled tying twine or cut through stubborn, half-cut sheaves with scythes. They then arranged the sheaves into stooks, to dry before threshing. From a distance the stooks looked like people. A growing population out in the big open. Contemplating the sun, the warmth, the quiet.

Each day they worked past dusk, stopping for a brief lunch of bread and cheese, until they could no longer see what lay before them. Evenings, when they came in from the fields and took their places at their outdoor table, Una slipped in beside Abel on the bench.

One night, Lucie pan-fried venison steaks for everyone. He had not eaten anything so tender and delicious in a long time. As he swallowed, with Una so near their elbows touched—his friends laughing, faces lit by a candle's shaft of light—his eyes and nose began to sting. The last time he'd cried, he was kneeling next to his dead father. But the tears coming now were different. This was happiness, maybe. Or something close to it. He was grateful no one could see in the dark.

After putting the children to sleep, Lucie brought out steaming rose milk pudding and asked Abel to make coffee since Una's, she said, was undrinkable. They ate, then built a pit fire. While Cy played a berceuse on his fiddle, Toby came out in his pyjamas, clutching the knight Merle had carved for him. He crawled into his mother's lap. "Who was the best warrior?"

"Lance." Merle added wood to the fire.

"Lancelot was certainly the favourite," Una said. "Always off on his reckless exploits. But I'm not sure he had more than his self-interest at heart." She brushed the boy's hair from his eyes. "I always preferred Arthur's dignified reserve. He was the brave one, protecting Britain. He stayed loyal to his people. And to his queen."

Toby yawned. "Arthur's boring."

"But he was constant," Lucie reached out, tickling Toby's bare foot, "in his convictions."

"Unlike that sinner la reine Guenièvre." Cy set down his bow and fiddle.

Una watched the flames dance. "You know, in some stories, Guinevere loved only Arthur, and found Lancelot brutish." She glanced at Abel. "But Arthur was too caught up in his morals to see how she felt." She pulled Toby off her lap and led him inside.

Abel sprang up. Did she feel something too, then? Or was he imagining a message where there was none? He wanted to follow her in but found himself unable to move. Mistaking his intention, everyone else rose too, and said goodnight, Merle shuffling into the farmhouse and the Peloquins into the bunkhouse.

He stood there until his shadow died with the fire, then crossed the fields between their houses. Midway, he turned back to see Una at her bedroom window. In a signal he hoped she would understand, he raised his lantern high, until the wind blew it out.

After checking on Tansy and Elizabeth Moon, he went inside and settled on his mattress on the living room floor. He was so anxious for morning to come that he couldn't sleep. The moon glowed through the curtains, a ring radiating around it. When he lay on his left side, his heart pounded in his ears. On his right side, the pulse was less loud.

The harvest took under three weeks.

After binding, the hot sun cured the stooks fast and Abel drove his thresher, powered by the tractor, to the Wisharts. He and his friends fed the sheaves into the machine, which separated the grain from the straw in no time.

While Cy and his children stayed behind to move and store the straw stacks left in the fields, Abel helped transport the grain to the elevators with Una and Merle. The two remaining elevators had been reinforced with bracing, and had reopened in July. Other farmers lined up there too—men Abel had not seen in years.

The Wisharts' grain was weighed, inspected and graded. From the wagon their load was augered into a hopper and lifted by conveyor belt into the elevator. It took many trips to unload all the grain. Once they received payment, Abel's neighbours parted ways with him so they could fetch Toby and freshen up before making the drive to Sterling to see Harold Nettles.

On their way back from the bank, they stopped to visit Abel. Merle and Toby waited in the truck Lewis had found them—far superior to the rattletrap Abel had restored—while Una ran over to where he was grinding out cracks in the binder.

"It's done," she said with a sunburnt smile. "We're fine another year. Though with none to spare."

The tension he had held so long in his neck and shoulders dissipated then. His body felt a hundred pounds lighter, and when he laughed he heard his father's laughter coming out from deep within.

"Oh! You haven't sounded like that...since Miss Kitty. I always envied her"—Una put a hand on her forehead to shield her eyes against the sun—"knowing how to make you laugh. Lord knows I tried."

"You did?"

She looked toward his house. "I was thinking we should plant poplars. A long line between our farms. To protect us from the elements. But then..." She turned to him. "I wouldn't see you. And you wouldn't see me."

Merle and Toby got out of the truck and walked over.

Toby ran circles around Abel. "You find your fool's gold yet?"

"Toby, hush!" Una sent him skipping back to the truck.

"You did us a great service." Merle extended a hand. "When can we return the favour?"

Summer, 1939

The Wisharts still had a lot to do before the cold set in. They needed these weeks to turn the soil and plant winter wheat in fallow rows. They couldn't waste time in case snow came early.

"I prefer working alone," he told them.

Una was still studying his house. As she walked past him, Abel felt as if a horseshoe was being pitched through his insides. He waited with Merle, who knelt to tie the catgut strings of his boots.

When she returned, the colour had drained from her complexion. "Where has the backside gone?" Her voice was hoarse. "We thought you were pilfering from First Street."

Merle rested a hand on his buckle. "I knew what he was up to."

"You tore your house down to keep us warm?"

"I'm rebuilding."

If Una had noticed what he was doing, she would have refused the wood. Unlike most farmers in these parts, who built their homes in the centre of their properties, Abel's father had wanted to step out of the front door and see their fields spread out before them. There were no roads behind the house, only unbroken grassland. The Wisharts, the schoolhouse and Grayley all lay in the other direction, and it had been dark when everyone came for the barn dance.

Abel filed the binder. "What do I need two bedrooms for?"

"You just never know," her chin twitched, "what you may need two bedrooms for."

Merle put a hand on his shoulder. "Don't be shy to give us a holler."

Abel nodded, and the old man left them. Una waited. But he was having difficulty speaking again. No words would come.

"Well. Goodbye then," she finally said and walked away. Then she rushed back over and took his hand. She leaned in and kissed him on the cheek. "Thank you."

He imagined kneeling before her, kissing her fingertips. Wait, he told himself. Not yet. After a few seconds, she let go, walked back to the truck and drove home to her shorn fields.

That evening he opened the Hoosier cabinet drawer and pulled out a small cardboard box. Inside were his parents' wedding bands. They still gave off a dull glow. He wrapped the rings in a handkerchief and slipped them in his pocket.

He sat in the rocker and turned on the radio, tuning in to Mackenzie King pledging that if there was a war there would be no conscription—that Canada's support would be to provide supplies, food and munitions.

Abel had already purchased his rapeseed and stowed the bags in the barn for the next sowing season. In a year, acres of flowers would give way to seed pods, to be harvested and processed into oil. Closing his eyes, he pictured Una first laying eyes on the millions of tiny blooms, yellowest of yellow, with petals the size of her pinky nail.

He spent the next several days cleaning the binder and thresher, replacing worn chains and greasing both machines. Whistling while he worked, he imagined Una as a bride. Maybe they could marry in the schoolhouse, and decorate it as they had decorated for the king and queen. He thought how Toby might come to love him, and all the stories Merle would recount about his early years ranching when they sat together evenings. He imagined their growing family.

Abel was in the barn when rain blew in, with lightning and thunder, falling heavier by the minute. He filled buckets with water—lately the sudden showers were quick and harmless—but the rain did not let up. All the rain he had wished for in the last ten years came down now, pummelling his crops. The wheat lost its lustre and the fields turned muddy, and still the rain fell, until no heavy machinery would be able to operate without getting stuck.

The sun will be hot tomorrow, he told himself. The crops will rebound. We've been through worse before.

The temperature dropped. Hail fell with the rain, increasing in size from pellets to eggs to baseballs within seconds. The chickens, caught off guard, rushed in circles in the yard rather than seeking

Summer, 1939

shelter. Shielding his head with his arms, Abel ran to the coop to usher them to safety, but two lay dead in the run. The hail pounded his back like a fist. He rushed to the stable, where Tansy and Elizabeth Moon bowed their heads in their stalls as the hail pelted the roof. "We'll be okay." He used his father's lie. "Gather close."

Within minutes the drumming and clattering ended. All was quiet.

Rubbing the bumps on his arms, he opened the stable door and looked out at his flattened fields. The hail was already melting. He picked ice balls up, hurling them as far as he could, toward the railway line. He couldn't eat his chickens, he couldn't bring himself to pluck the feathers from their warm bodies. Instead he dug two small graves in an open patch by the paddock, buried his hens and returned to the house.

Una came as the sun set and a band of pink pushed against the dark clouds.

When he opened the door, she walked right in. "It's my fault," she said. "We're the ones who should be ruined. Not you."

"Th-there's always next year." He took his hat and led her outside.

"Harold will extend your loans, then?"

"Always does."

"Alright." She nodded. "But, Abel. You'll let us know. If we can—"

"I'll— let you know."

He followed her to the edge of his field and stopped there.

How could he have mistaken her affections. The look on her face now was one of pity. "I'll see you," he told her, and left her to walk home in the storm's afterglow. He did not even watch her go.

*On this last journey,
what the queen told the mare
of undying love goes unspoken.*
—A.D.

22

Seven days in a row Lewis Lyte appeared at the Wisharts'. It made Abel think of that song the Peloquins sang, about the prince visiting a house each day of the week. Monday, Tuesday, Wednesday, all the way to Sunday. Returning and persisting.

The visits were lengthy, distracting Abel from his clean-up. Whenever he looked across the fields, there was Lewis. Playing in the yard with Toby. Bringing supplies in. Stacking a cord of wood obtained from god knew where. On one occasion he even showed up in his Red Serge rather than in his usual brown tunic. Looking like a smear of blood in the distance.

Eventually he came over to where Abel was wading through pools of water, examining shredded stems and clearing out his losses. His fields were still wet. His wheat had turned to rot. As for the kernels that didn't rot, they swelled and sprouted, rendering the wheat worthless even as feed. When Merle had come to lend a hand, Abel had sent him away. There would be no yield. The growing season was too short to start again. This wasn't something he would recover from.

"Tough break." Lewis leaned against a fencepost. "What'll you do?"

"I'll get by."

Lewis showed Abel his new shoulder board, three stripes beneath a crown. He had been promoted to sergeant.

When Abel congratulated him, a muscle in Lewis's jaw contracted. His eyes went watery as he removed his wide-brimmed hat. "I'm asking her to marry me." He blinked as he looked over at the Wisharts' farm, then took in Abel's beaten fields. "Now that I can provide."

Abel fixed on Lewis's hair. He wondered how he kept it so shiny. His whole head was like polished brass. Then Abel picked up his shovel and started digging.

"I'll be off, then." Lewis put his hat back on. "Good luck to you, Dodds." Returning to his car, he didn't seem to mind that his tall black service boots got covered in mud. As he drove off, he gave a joyous honk, three blasts.

Abel looked down the fence line he had built with his father, delineating wheatfields from pastureland. What did he need a fence for anymore?

He went to the shed for cutters and gloves. Returning to the entry point of the fence by the road, he cut the wire. The wood posts came out of the loose mud easily, one by one. They were like fangs biting down on the prairie. Creating divisions where there should be none. Laying claim on a vast expanse that could not be owned.

It took two days to free the land. Pulling up each post, Abel ran the length of his arm into the holes, feeling around the muck, coming up empty handed. The posts, he cut and stacked into piles to dry in the barn for the coming winter. Since Jake had not come home.

Summer, 1939

Toby wandered over while Abel was still digging, making holes everywhere. He couldn't stop. Even though his hands were bleeding, his shoulders gave off sharp pains, and his stab wound pulsated.

The boy crouched, looking into a small crater. "Anything?"

Abel dropped his shovel.

"I'll find your gold." Toby picked up the shovel and pushed his small boot down on the blade. "Just you wait."

"What about school?"

"What about it?"

"Someone around here's— got to learn."

"Lewis says I don't have to go anymore." He flung a little mud aside. "At least not to this rotten place."

"We learned— a lot in that schoolhouse. Me and your mom."

"Lewis says he'll drive me to the city."

"Every day?"

"Not every day. Some days." He pulled a wrinkled square of fabric from his pocket and pressed it against Abel's stomach. "You're bleeding." Abel looked down and put his hand over the handkerchief embroidered with her initials. The boy stepped away. "You're welcome to it. Lewis got us new ones."

A swallow dove into a mud hole. Blue like sapphire. They watched it struggle and flit in the damp hollow, before setting itself free.

In the evening he listened to "Moonlight Sonata" on the gramophone. Then to the news of Hitler invading Poland. Two days later, France and Britain declared war on Germany. The following week, when Canada joined Britain, Abel took a slow ride out with Tansy, to the place where they'd sat with the king and queen.

The wild roses, for the most part, had lost their scent. A few were still open but wilted, the spot where he had set down the quilt covered in thorn and thistle. He rested there anyway.

Lying on his back, he thought about the Royal Train, hauling the couple to appear before millions of people. King George and Queen Elizabeth had united a divided country. City and rural folk, the wealthy and the poor, anglophones and francophones, formed a bond. Even those who had not seen their majesties learned about the tour through the radio and newspapers, or local lore—people living in the far North or on remote islands, those on traplines or logging in forests, immigrant families on outlying farms or crews underground in mines, prisoners and patients in isolation, bush pilots and one-room-schoolhouse teachers, labourers and factory workers, whalers and wilderness guides, housewives and ranchers—all had the tour in common. Canada's loyalty had gone from wavering to fierce, many communities now keen to join the war.

Abel sat up. Soon the surrounding bushes would produce rose-hips. Thousands upon thousands of hard, red berries. Who in their lifetime could say that they had picnicked with the king and queen? That was something to remember always. Even if the king and queen hadn't been there—if it had been only him and Una—his life, in that moment, would have felt complete.

He knew now that some things, such as weather, occurred without agency or malice. And people must adapt.

He stood and massaged Tansy's neck and shoulders. "What did she tell you?" His mare lowered her head as if readying herself for a good long sleep. As if to say, *It's alright. Everything is as it should be.*

Together they journeyed homeward.

That night he played no records, tuning into news broadcasts. Reports mainly highlighted King George and Queen Elizabeth's reaction to Canada joining their ranks. They were grateful, they were proud, they were moved by the Commonwealth. They would stay in London, they would not flee. From Buckingham Palace, the queen expressed her love and gratitude to all Canadians.

Summer, 1939

His trip to Sterling was Tansy's last ride. He'd run out of gas — he didn't want to go by truck anyway, preferring to travel with her without rushing. How long had he dreaded this day? Only, now that it had finally arrived, he found himself entering the bank with ease and telling Harold Nettles, "I'm ready. To let it all go." And Harold did not argue.

Signing the papers was liberating. As though he were freeing his father, his mother, himself. Freeing the prairie, even. Harold pointing all the while, with "Your signature, please. Here, and here. And here."

In the city he made one more stop, at the jeweller rumoured to have the gift of conjuring diamonds from water and melting corn into gold. Inside, Abel pulled out the few banknotes he had just received, adding his parents' wedding bands, his father's pocket watch and his mother's locket to the pile on the countertop. He asked the old man, "Can you make gold from these?"

Returning home along the rail line, Abel and Tansy stopped to collect coal.

Though the cold was coming, all around the barn, John McCrae's cosmos now bloomed.

Tansy was in pain.

Abel felt her wincing with each step. She couldn't canter and no longer grazed. She couldn't lie down, or rise, without him.

He gave her some of the Peloquins' carrots, cool water and a peppermint. He brushed her coat and leaned his forehead against hers. He listened to her laboured breathing.

She followed him out to the flowers behind the barn — how those white buds from the Boer War had spread! — and once she was no longer anxious, but calmed, Abel put his rifle against her forehead and discharged a bullet.

As she fell to the ground her limbs twitched only a little. He pressed his ear against her still-warm coat, to make sure her heart had stopped beating. Then he walked the fields for what felt like an eternity, until he found a torn drift of silk laid out across the land like a shroud. Bringing the parachute back to Tansy, he covered her, and lit his mare's body on fire.

The next day he rose before dawn to feed the chickens and Elizabeth Moon. Tansy's bridle he left hanging on its peg in the stable.

He ate his porridge, cleaned the kitchen and put his parents' wedding photo and a few other things into his pack. Then he peeled back the last walls of his home — all but one — adding the wood to the stack in the barn.

The house his father had built was a dollhouse open to the world. A roof on a frame, and a front facade. A floor with a door and two open windows, whose pillowcase curtains fluttered in the prairie breeze. The kitchen window had the best view southeast, onto a whitewashed schoolhouse and neighbour's farm. Two winged pigs on the sill, and a stone feather that Abel put in his pocket.

He filled the old buckboard with seed bags, provisions, a shovel. Pulling the cart from his property down the road to the Wisharts', he surveyed their tidy fields, ready for planting. Rapeseed would do well here.

Finding a spot where he might have looked for gold as a child, he dug a hole, burying treasure for a boy to find. Setting the cart by the bunkhouse, he sat and looked out at his farm and the schoolhouse brightening in the distance.

Toby came out with an egg basket then. When he saw Abel, he came over to where he sat. "Where are you going?"

"On a train ride," Abel said. "I've never b-been east before. I'd like to see that — part of the country."

"Like the king and queen."

He nodded. "Only my a-accommodations won't be so grand."

"You're talkin' funny again."

"I suppose so."

"Those must be great." He eyed his binoculars. "To look at hawks and things."

Summer, 1939

"Keep my— going a secret"—Abel handed them over—"and they're yours."

Toby put the binoculars around his neck. "They're heavy."

"You'll g-get used to the heaviness. After a while."

Toby focused north. "What happened to your house?"

"It fell."

"Mom says you're rebuilding. And burning acres to start clean. Where is your horse?"

"Out to pasture."

"Can we have your cow?"

"She's dried out."

"We'll slaughter her."

"Let her graze. You can— kill the chickens. There's wood in the barn."

The boy nodded.

"I was scouting the wrong— area," he added. "The g-gold's here."

Toby's eyes widened. "On our farm?"

"You ought to— keep looking." He pulled a dog-eared book from his bag, handing it over. "That's for you."

Toby flipped through the pages. "What's an idyll?"

"An— idyll's a place like a poem."

"Like here?"

"Sometimes."

Toby opened at random. "Rain, sun, and rain! and the free blossom blows: Sun, rain, and sun! and where is he who knows?" The corners of his mouth lifted. He turned to another page. "I know thee for my King!... Sware on the field of death a deathless love." He giggled. "It's a bit silly. Are there tournaments?"

Abel nodded. "There's— jousting."

Toby dropped the book in his coat pocket. "Will you come back?"

"Maybe."

"Send me a postcard?"

"I'll try." Abel rose, and they walked back to the farmhouse.

As they went in, Una looked up and dropped her tea towel. "Oh! It's you." She returned to staring at the radio with Merle, listening to the latest report about volunteers signing up to serve overseas. The Royal Tour all but forgotten.

She looked into her son's basket. "Where are my eggs?"

Toby ran back outside.

Abel sat with Merle while the news droned on. "It won't last." Merle lit his pipe. "After a few months it'll be done." The way he said it, glancing at his granddaughter with a strained smile, Abel understood these as empty words for the sake of comfort.

Abel rose and went to the kitchen where she was washing a pan. "Una," he said. "I'm— going to show you how to make— coffee now."

Fall 1939

In courage you found joy
and triumphed over rainless lands.
I think of your hands a lot
in my rainy kingdom.
—A.D.

23

So no one would see him depart from the Grayley platform he walked further west, in the opposite direction of where he would eventually be going. Travelling without Tansy felt strange.

The walk was long but he was in no hurry. He stopped at the cemetery and set the feather stone between his parents' graves. He found the wolf's bones from winter, and stayed there awhile. Then he continued on to the city and boarded the train in Sterling. From there he passed everything in reverse. The abandoned farms and tarpaper shacks, the riverbed where water again flowed. The two Wise Men and the station, Grayley and its burnt church and hall, his farmstead and the schoolhouse of his youth and the Wishart farm. How funny to see it all from this perspective! No one came out to wave. Why would they, having no notion he was riding by? He observed his old life with some awe, as one would a sunset, until it dimmed beyond comprehension.

The train went fast as a go-devil sleigh, passing the Peloquins' flung-open door. In a fleeting glimpse, he caught sight of the railcar's insides, stripped bare. The Peloquins weren't ones for goodbyes either. Like him, they had left abruptly. All the swallows had departed, too. The day before, he had watched them scatter like a bucket of blue shards tossed into the sky. Leaving it an empty chalk white.

On he went, eastward, like the starving jobless men in their failed On-to-Ottawa Trek. Eastward like the king and queen going home. Riding the way tens of thousands of soldiers would soon go, through the golden glow of Alberta, Saskatchewan, Manitoba, past innumerable farmsteads like his, so many he lost count. He felt he was seeing the life he might have had flash before him again and again and again, like a flip book. In his mind he sketched Una, Toby and Merle inside the book with him. They appeared together, like ghosts on the plains in front of this farm or that farm, in front of windmills, water towers, ranches, stubble fields and haystacks, all the way to Ontario, where farms were replaced by factories.

There would be jobs in Ontario now. But Abel had explored other occupations during the off seasons. The prospect of warehouse labour or assembly-line tasks was an anvil on his chest, weighing him down until he couldn't breathe. Besides, the pay was too poor to get by, and where would he sleep?

He continued on until Ottawa.

Up the street from the station, he visited the war memorial the king and queen had christened. The mythic figures were impressive. The stone seemed to ripple in the wind, the drapery and detailing majestic. His father, he thought, would have appreciated such fine sculpting.

From the memorial he walked up to Parliament Hill. The gothic centre block on its limestone bluffs overlooking the river, and the Peace Tower, were grand. Standing before the austere government buildings with other tourists, hat in hand, he enquired after the

Fall, 1939

prime minister. But the guard said Mackenzie King wasn't there. The House was not in session.

Back at the station, he ate a piece of raisin pie. Terrible pie he couldn't swallow. Then he boarded the train again and it carried him, beneath a plume of black smoke, through Quebec and New Brunswick. He continued by rail and ferry to Nova Scotia, the departure point for soldiers bound for the Atlantic front.

In Halifax he found a public bathhouse, where he cleaned himself up. Afterwards he went for a lunch of chops and pea soup. Then he got a haircut, drank two pints in a beer parlour and enlisted. Although his stutter had returned, he hid it by not speaking much. After he passed the medical exams and was officially considered suitable for service, Abel gave his oath of allegiance to serve King George VI as long as was deemed necessary by His Majesty.

At Camp Aldershot he excelled at basic training—at the drills, heavy lifting and early morning risings. It wasn't hard. Most of the men weren't men but boys who lied about their age. Out-of-work fellows desperate for a hot meal and a bed. Young men whose wives would now receive government checks.

From September until May he trained in the artillery, while nothing much seemed to be happening overseas. They called this time the phoney war. The twilight war. The sitting war. The bore war.

Running through marksmanship exercises and cleaning rifles, Abel didn't think about who had taken over his father's farm, or whether Una and Lewis had wed. But he did wonder if she had planted the rapeseed.

Sometimes he thought he smelled the prairie earth and fresh grasses from the base. Sometimes he could see hawks in the wind, and feel the spring breezes on his skin—even in the damp of a Maritime winter.

Almost a year to the day the king and queen had passed through Grayley, Germany stepped up their invasions. Winston Churchill, who was all for a fight, took over from Chamberlain, and Canada was suddenly needed. Abel's unit, along with a dozen others, set sail for Great Britain.

On the Atlantic crossing, he thought of the royal fleet that had not long ago voyaged in the opposite direction. And how England had sent vessels weighted with gold bars that could have helped the whole Dominion back on its feet, and how those bars remained hidden in vaults, until they would be needed to fund battles.

"You're taking a simplistic view of things," his father said. "Seems straightforward enough to me," Abel replied. More and more lately, he found his father next to him. They debated the true reason for Abel's enlistment. "I had no other options," he told Gilly Dodds. "Son, you did it to be part of something larger than yourself." Abel said that was hogwash. "Whatever the case," his father added, "might as well apply yourself now that you're here. As you always have." Abel thought this through. "Yes, dad. I will."

Ten days later, the units of soldiers disembarked in Liverpool and moved on to their respective training facilities.

Abel and hundreds of men took a train to their base near the dank Salisbury Plain. Drill grounds were cold and muddy. The barracks were packed beyond capacity, housing thousands of extra British and Canadian troops. They practised with obsolete weapons, learning how to wage trench warfare. At this point, Abel realized that most of the Canadian men there—those who had already suffered through a winter on the Plain—had arrived without even basic training.

They arm wrestled, and held tug-of-war contests and boxing matches, as they had in their boyhoods back home. Most came from the prairies and had lost everything. They discussed the invasion of France, the Dunkirk Evacuation and the unfolding Battle of Britain,

Fall, 1939

and how Italy would suffer for joining the Axis, and oh, how Hitler would pay.

In August, on a day's leave, Abel went to London for the first time.

He wanted to visit the British Museum. But all the museums were closed, emptied of their contents. He sent Toby a postcard from a tobacco shop, with a picture of a suit of armour on a stand. In a café overlooking the Thames, he wrote to Una. And sealed his letter in an envelope marked Royal Mail. Then tore it up.

A few weeks later, the Luftwaffe attacked London.

Aerial bombings of Britain's towns and cities went on for several months, night and day, until the following May, and still Abel's unit awaited deployment. The boys complained. They wanted to see action. Abel said nothing. He got reassigned twice, to fill vacancies in new units. He excelled at drills, marching, tactics and procedures and physical fitness tests, and was promoted to second lieutenant. Being responsible for the lives of other men weighed on him. "Try not to worry," his father said.

How to account for the next year that passed? When hours and days galloped and then slowed imperceptibly. It reminded him of Tansy's fluid movement, and of harvest time, when sleep and dream and work felt as one.

When he had leave, he took the train to London to build up his tolerance, until the whirlwind of uniformed soldiers, automobiles, lights, racket and pollution no longer gave him headaches.

All that rubble. All those bombed-out buildings. The Palace of Westminster, Buckingham Palace, the Tower of London and the British Museum were all hit. Some neighbourhoods had been entirely destroyed.

On these visits he took to standing in front of the Houses of Parliament. Though damaged, Big Ben still resembled Canada's

Peace Tower. He went to Buckingham Palace. Contemplating the limestone building through the ornamental iron fence, he determined that if their majesties came out, he would tell them that he admired their sticking around, not fleeing to their countryside residence where it was safe, like many in their position would have done.

It was hard to believe that the king and queen had been in Canada. That they had come to Grayley and that Abel had been there too, among those impossible blooms. So close to his former schoolmate that he could have reached out and kissed her, and professed whatever it was that all his life had consumed him.

Now here he was at the gates of the palace, and she in the fields back home. The world was embroiled in another war. And what was real and what was imagined blurred.

In a pub one day, a familiar voice called his name.

"Lordy lord, it's Abel Dodds. Look at you in that fine getup! Or I suppose I ought to call you sir. Bet you don't recognize me, do you, sir?" He turned to his comrades. "Look here, fellas! He's the one who got me to clean up my errant ways."

Abel would have recognized the rakish grin anywhere, whether in a drifter's torn clothes or a soldier's crisp uniform. As it turned out, Abel and Freddie Teel were stationed on the same base. Lifting his shirt, Abel showed his jagged scar from the wound which, touched by her handkerchief, had healed. "You owe me a drink." He joined Freddie and his friends at the table.

Freddie bought Abel pints of stout all night. Abel learned that after their encounter in Sterling, Freddie had gotten himself a job at a livery. But that only lasted so long. Even so, he kept out of trouble, stopped riding the rails and made peace with his losses.

"You're the last one I thought I'd see here." Freddie chewed on a toothpick. "You never struck me as...a fighter."

Abel supposed he should tell Freddie that he was fighting for democracy. Most of the men who had come from his part of the world told him they were there because they had nowhere else to go. This was their way out of the depression.

Fall, 1939

How could he explain that he was not sacrificing himself for any greater good, but that he was fighting for his neighbours. He had not given up on home. He was saving every dollar earned, he would return one day and try again.

The boys held their pints of dark ale in the air, spilling them and vowing to destroy the moustached devil wanting to take over the world. Toasting and gulping.

Freddie often tracked Abel down on the base, following him around the mess hall, the sports fields and barracks.

Sometimes they talked late into the night. Other times they went to London to help clear rubble or walk along the Thames, feeding bread to dirty swans.

They spent evenings in underground, windowless clubs where jazz bands drowned out air raid sirens and where the girls wore backless, beaded gowns. Abel never sought out a girl's company, despite Freddie's coaxing. The young man finally blurted, "Look, sir, if you're homosexual just say it, I won't mind, I had an uncle who—"

Abel cut him off. He'd had just enough drink to say, "There was someone."

Freddie dragged him away from the raw cry of the saxophone, its notes everlasting. "Spill the beans," he said as they lit smokes in the alley. To amuse his companion, Abel invented a story about a girl from a place that did not exist.

When brain spills from face
and voice breaks from spleen,
pink blooms reign over sky
that is both our eternity.
—*A.D.*

24

In July he was informed by his commanding officer that his unit would be participating in a secret raid. Around that time, a letter came. *Would you believe*, it said, *Toby found gold out by the well.* The ink blotted halfway down the page, over scribbled-out words. Then, further down, *I had Lewis find you for me. He told me you enlisted. Why did you not say goodbye?*

The date and postmark were old. She had written while he was still in Halifax. For nearly two years the letter had been lost, and rerouted.

Of course he knew that the gold he buried would be found at once. It had to be, the way he'd put it under a mound with a little shine sticking out, leaving a spade nearby. But he hadn't expected any expression of emotion from her. It was possible, then. It was possible that they felt the same way.

His laughter came out as a howl.

By now she would be married. By now she and Lewis would have children. By now he would be forgotten. He kept her letter in his breast pocket.

He even wrote back. A poem of four lines he composed without pause or hesitation. He imagined posting it in the Royal Mail. Imagined it travelling across the ocean on a steel liner, then across the country by train, following the flow of the Horseshoe River, to his home, as the king and queen had done. And he thought about what his lines might ignite between them, and how some things came too late. For a while he thought about the poet John McCrae, and wondered whether he had ever sat by the Thames as Abel did now.

Rising to go, he straightened his uniform. He left the poem on the bench for the ravenous swans.

On August 18, more than six thousand troops, including Abel's unit, set sail for the raid on the French seaside town of Dieppe. Freddie was eager to fight Germany. He told Abel he would cut off Nazi ears. That he would bring the enemy to her knees and choke her. Abel reminded him of the Geneva Convention, but Freddie scoffed and kissed Abel on both cheeks. "Here we go!" And off he went to join his squad.

The engagement was called Operation Jubilee.

Dieppe was a casino town. The men joked that after they got the Krauts they would gamble and drink French champagne, and meet pretty French girls. So as not to be seen by the enemy, they crossed the Channel from the south, heading toward France before the next day's dawn. As they approached the shore, their major-general told them that it would be a piece of cake.

Only, they were delayed by twenty minutes. With daylight arriving, German defenders saw them coming.

By the time the ramp went down and troops stormed the beach, the Germans were ready. Abel and his men found themselves pinned against the seawall, unable to advance as machine-gun fire rained down from the cliffs above.

Fall, 1939

He watched dozens gunned down in minutes. Allied aircraft fell burning from the sky. The ships that had carried them in began retreating, and where were the Churchill tanks that were supposed to have landed already, to protect them?

Around him, men abandoned their posts, running toward the village or down the beach, into the sea. He couldn't locate anyplace safe inside the smoke and noise. The pebbles were like quicksand. He dragged bodies back against the seawall because it was all he could do.

Amid the chaos and bullets and choking thirst, he thought of the water pail at the schoolhouse entryway. A tin pail and dipper with a deep round bowl, the school bell ringing, clouds casting drifts of shadow over the fields as he ran to the Dutch door, how cool and fresh that water tasted! He had never drunk anything more delicious, that day she stood waiting with the long-handled ladle, and poured water into his cupped hands the last warm week of school. That same week she passed a poem to him over her shoulder, written on a scrap of paper, *Roses are pink / the sky is blue / spring is sweet / as are you.* How incensed he was at the time, thinking she mocked him! Even so, on the other side of that scrap he wrote a verse too, intending to pass it back. Only he never got it right—erasing and rewriting and erasing twenty-three pocket poems over the years—until the paper thinned and his sweaty hands smudged her message, and the eraser tore through. And there was Freddie Teel charging, baring his teeth, shouting god knew what. Then he was hit.

Abel dragged him behind a pile of mooring sinkers.

Protected by the concrete blocks, Freddie spat blood and said something Abel couldn't hear. Something that sounded like, "Kiss me, sissy," with that boyish grin, but in his eyes, terror. His intestines spilling out. He gripped Abel's hand, and this time Abel heard him clearly. "Tell 'em back— home. I made it t-to the theatre."

Home. Back home they would be harvesting. The fields would be golden, the rapeseed would have already bloomed its shock of vibrant yellow, its flowering time done. And the sky. Oh the sky sky

sky! But it was blue here too. Abel saw blue above the smoke when the tanks finally landed and rolled forward, driven by farm boys who could operate big machinery, only their tracks were filling up with rocks, the tanks getting stuck on the shoreline as their belts snapped.

"You're too late!" Frantic, Abel gestured for the armoured vehicles to go back to the ships. The tanks were hit. Men climbed out of the hatches, flinging themselves on the banks, their clothes and skin engulfed in flame. Soon Abel could hear nothing over the roar of the machines and planes and firepower. He lost sight of where Freddie lay. He stopped counting casualties — couldn't understand his captain's hollered orders over the blasts. This went on for hours.

He found a shell hole the size of a grain bin, on the beach. Pressed his face against the side of the crater's sand and pebbles, as he once rested his cheek on Elizabeth Moon's warm body, positioning himself by her udder to milk on winter mornings. She didn't mind, her calm breathing a comfort in the biting air, breath coming out in puffs of steam. Without this routine, the day had felt incomplete. Streams of milk hitting the pail, snow landing in a thin layer over the yard outside the barn, clouds going so quick from purple to pink to white, if you looked away a moment you missed the show.

A mortar landed at his feet. It didn't detonate but rolled away. Abel groped for the dud round to hurl it out but couldn't find it in the sand, pebbles and mud. Peering over the edge of his hideout, he glimpsed two Germans. A commanding officer was yelling at a private.

The private kicked a body nearby, knelt and rifled through the pockets. He pulled out a letter and photograph. A lighter and cigarettes. Opened the letter then showed the photograph to his officer. Laughed, made a lewd gesture. Burned it and dropped it on the body, keeping the lighter and cigarettes. His officer turned to go, turned back, aimed at the private's chest and shot him. The private fell forward and landed by Abel's hole, head twisted to the side,

Fall, 1939

eyes blinking over and over. Then he saw Una. She was a queen, with roses in her hair. They'd had seasons together. An interluce. A period of stillness, when they were all royalty and noblemen and ladies and knights and magicians.

No one was left on the beach.

He crawled out of his hole but found he couldn't walk, his uniform heavy with blood. He lay down on the cobblestones, heart slowing.

He thought about how he had recited poetry to the animals in the barn, sitting on a bale of hay as they ate.

But now farewell. I am going a long way . . . / Where falls not hail, or rain, or any snow, / Nor ever wind blows loudly . . . / Where I will heal me of my grievous wound.

His father stood at the barn door and clapped. A few cows mooed.

"Do you reckon our fates are— written?" he once asked Gilly Dodds on a trip to Sterling. They transported milk, butter, cheese and a crate of baby chicks. Their wagon went slow along the lone road crossing the land. The milk tins rattled and the chicks in their wire container lined with wood shavings made soft, high-pitched cheeps.

His father chirruped the horses. "Best you can do's love and be fearless."

He had not answered the question. Abel nodded.

They rode past a field of sunflowers. The heads of the flowers on their tall stalks turned and turned, following their journey.

25

May 1943

Dear sister,

I write from an estate in the English countryside. Such places are being offered up by their owners to be used as hospitals. Some say this one belongs to nobles related to the king.

I don't know what day it is anymore and can't be bothered to ask.

I know it's May because the magnolia trees are in bloom. I know I miss Toby, despite what you think. And I know I'm grateful that he's under your care, and what a better mother you have been to him than I could have.

Sometimes I still smell that smell he had when he was born, like sweet, ripe wheat. Closing my eyes I see home and a sea of seed heads nodding on the stem all the way to infinity.

They say the war will end soon but I think that's wishful thinking.

I thought it would be an adventure here on the front. I had a romantic vision of things. Like our brash brother. Jake's chasing his cowboy dreams till conscription ropes him in.

THIS BRIGHT DUST

You were right, though, sister. It was thoughtless of me to take all we had for granted. Back then I felt we had nothing and it infuriated me. I wish I was like you, and saw the goodness and fullness in everything. I suppose that's how you've endured. Thinking about you now, Una Maeve, I realize you're the most complex one of us all—that you keep hidden what's truly thumping and bumping around inside you, and my admiration for you grows. Out here I think, be like Una. See the bright side.

We sleep three hours a night. One day bleeds into the next. I have a story to tell.

From what I understand, back home the stories about Dieppe are different.

Back home I heard that at first they said the raid was a success. It was a disaster. Oh, Una. The things I've seen. The flesh that peels off in my hands.

There I was just off the boat with my nursing sisters, and they send me to this big old country house for the wounded who made it out of the casualty clearing stations by the docks and railways.

This is what we do here. We go from mansion to mansion with corpses.

I digress. As you know by now if gramps still blares the radio, close to a thousand of ours were killed, and thousands more were taken prisoner and put in camps. The chief surgeon told me, "You get to take care of the lucky ones."

A lot of the lucky ones had no faces or fingers. The lucky ones couldn't speak, see or hear, and stank like burnt flesh and excrement.

So there I was, a novice in death, surrounded by all these lovely fellows in a stately home of five hundred beds. You can't imagine the groaning that went on. The echoing. But after a month I got used to it. Then one shift my trainer pulled me aside and told me, "Go to that one." *That one* always means it's going to be grim.

Fall, 1939

She said he was a second lieutenant who took over stretcher-bearing during the assault, and became a sort of live stretcher himself. He just kept running out, dragging men—even German dead—out of harm's way. When two privates found him right before the surrender, he'd been shot three times and was crawling out of a shell hole. They carried him unconscious to the last retreating ship.

He was a farmer from Alberta, she said, so I should be the one to take him.

Sitting down next to him, I could see right away how he was suffering, so I prepared the needle, only he pushed my hand away. I explained it was for pain. He got agitated and meanwhile the fellow in the next bed over called out for oblivion, so I gave it to him. When I returned to my patient, he said, "Una," and I said, "How do you know my sister?"

His face was torn up by mortar shell. When he spoke a few more words, that stern, deep voice—with a stammer like the king's—brought me straight back to the Grayley schoolyard, and some of us kids (not you of course) teasing, and I realized it was our neighbour Abel Dodds. Doleful Dodds! I almost blurted.

Instead I said, "It's me. Brynn Wishart."

It confused him. Seeing me. I explained how I'd decided to serve our country. Even if I may end up dead. He said, "Good. Good for you, Brynn." Then he said, "What about your sister?" He thought you wed that brick Lewis Lyte! I had a good laugh over that. I told him you'll never marry. All you ever wanted was to run the farm and that's what you're doing, and your rapeseed's growing in heaps and all's well with your world and Toby's, and with gramps. At my news his wretched face seemed to relax.

After our first encounter I would read to him.

He liked Tennyson, mostly, so dull it put us both to sleep. On mild days we went outside and I kept him supplied with flask and books. On good days he read a lot, and wrote, and tore up bits of paper. But on bad days he stayed lying in his bed and would go on about the execution of the Nazi. He wondered if the German officer who had killed the cruel Nazi was still alive. Haven't a clue what he meant by that. He never explained.

Sometimes we reminisced about Miss Kitty, and sometimes we talked about the great drought. One day I wondered aloud how many Canadians might have been saved had there been no royal visit — how many wouldn't have fought and died on the front for the Crown. And do you know what he answered? He said, it wouldn't have made any difference. The king and queen were responsible for leading Canadians to slaughter in the same way he himself was responsible for leading Freddie Teel to war.

I enquired who Freddie was, but he wouldn't say.

Where did blame begin and end, he asked. Who was willing and wanting, who had to go and who was forced to be here. Why not blame Mackenzie King, who kept his country so desperate they enlisted for a dollar a day. Maybe the fault lay with our prime minister. Or maybe it was human nature, to want to battle it out. He said it took him a long time to realize that. But that he was done with blaming.

I never told him of the rumours circulating, about how Lord Mountbatten and all of England knew this was a sacrifice, to kill Canada's soldiers off in a war that was just getting going. That the raid wasn't necessary. Who in their right mind would make a direct attack on the front line of a fortified port! Our men were killed off on that rocky beach for Great Britain to send a message to its allies, that it wasn't ready to invade occupied coastlines.

How dim-witted. Expressing my opinion for censors to black out.

We're told this is a war of necessity. They do love the Canucks here. Abel sometimes went on about the importance of protecting, through duty, all that we held dear in our hearts. I think that was for my benefit. Though he showed no sign of bitterness.

Fall, 1939

"What do you hold dear in your heart?" I asked him, and he said, "Your sister."

I think, Una, that Doleful Dodds had a crush on you!

Mostly he wanted to hear about the farm. How many bushels per acre. Had the schoolhouse reopened for Toby, were folks finally returning to Grayley (I lied and said yes), was an honest family living on his land (I didn't tell him how the elements turned it back to unbroken prairie, as you told me), how was Elizabeth Moon (I said fine. Is the cow fine?), and was Merle keeping out of trouble.

He also asked if the Peloquins came back. I didn't mention the two who enlisted and died the first year. I said I didn't know.

These conversations took place over a few months.

Sometimes it was too difficult for him to talk. So he wrote his thoughts out with his one good hand. I got the sense he preferred writing to speaking. Then he got a bad infection in his leg and they had to amputate. "Tell Freddie I made it to the theatre too," he wrote then, "to the operating theatre, ha."

Just before the procedure he asked the chief surgeon, "Do you know John McCrae? He's a doctor here."

The surgeon told him he had not had the privilege of meeting McCrae. He didn't say, that was the world war before ours. The first one we fought for England. I thought that pretty decent of him. Then he looked at me and remarked how we could do with some poetry around here.

This surgeon. His name is Roy. Sometimes we take comfort in each other. Don't be shocked, sister. It's a new era. He's a good fellow, and kind. I hope you find someone like him someday.

The last time I was with our neighbour, he wanted to go outside in the early morning even though it was miserably cold, and we could hear blasts in the distance. We'd have to move soon. I just knew it. But he wanted to go out into the damned field. He could be very persistent.

So off we went until he said we should stop. With his good

arm he reached over his chair and picked at the grass and dirt, smelling the clumps in his hand. There wasn't any sunrise, the sky was a sheet of grey. Then he said, "We saw them."

I asked who. He told me the king and queen. That you, sister, and he, picnicked with the king and queen of England. By a river of dust and roses.

How about that! I'm sure you did.

As I wheeled him back inside the sky lit up with reams of colour like streamers in a pavilion dance hall. I'd never seen anything like it and we both gasped. Then the clouds greyed again. "And they lived happily ever after," he said. As if the cover of a book had just closed.

A week later, some of us were moved from the estate, closer to the front line. I was one of the ones to go. When I went to say goodbye to Doleful Dodds, though, he was gone, his bed stripped bare.

I didn't cry or feel much, really. But I probed the new nurse looking as eager and terrified as I had when I first arrived, as to what happened.

She said he just died. He was dead when she found him.

They say he's buried in the Brookwood Military Cemetery not far from London, with other casualties from the raid, and commonwealth casualties from both wars. There's German and Italian prisoner plots there too. Maybe his German officer lies there. And that friend of his, Freddie Teel. He'd probably like that it stretches over acres and acres, all these graves growing forever across the plains.

For King and Country.

Anyway. I'm not writing to say I took care of him till his final breath or anything. I had other patients to attend to. I only wanted to say I saw him. I thought you would like to know. For a short while I served as his nurse. He asked after you.

Acknowledgements

During the writing of *This Bright Dust* the following books were indispensable: *The Great Depression: 1929–1939* by Pierre Berton, *Ten Lost Years, 1929–1939: Memories of the Canadians Who Survived the Depression* by Barry Broadfoot, *The Winter Years: The Depression on the Prairies* by James H. Gray, *Daylight Upon Magic: The Royal Tour of Canada, 1939* by Tom MacDonnell, and *Royalty Rides the Rails: A Railroading Perspective of the 1939 Canada/USA Royal Tour* by Larry Shaak.

Profound thanks to Samantha Haywood, Eva Oakes, Bethany Gibson. Gratitude also to Susanne Alexander, Julie Scriver, Alan Sheppard, Jeff Arbeau, Ben Burnett, Peter Norman, Destiny Chalifoux, and everyone at Goose Lane Editions. And to Farhad Kazemzadeh, Denise, Hans, Nadine Berkhout and Samuel Brown, always.

Nina Berkhout is the author of three previous novels, most recently *Why Birds Sing*, which was described as a "must read" by *the Globe and Mail*, a Best Book of the Year (Canada) by Audible, and a Great Group Reads selection by the Women's National Book Association (USA). Her young adult novel *The Mosaic* was nominated for the White Pine Award and named an Indigo Best Teen Book, and her novel *The Gallery of Lost Species* was named an Indigo and Kobo Best Book and a *Harper's Bazaar* Hottest Breakout Novel. Berkhout is also the author of five poetry collections, including *Elseworlds*, which won the Archibald Lampman Award. Her poems have been featured in publications across Canada including the *Best Canadian Poetry* anthology. Originally from Calgary, she lives in Ottawa.